Join Andie, Jina, Mary Beth, and Lauren
for more fun at the Riding Academy!

And coming soon:

She led Magic to the new barn. The overhead lights were on, but it was quiet. Stepping inside, she halted him in the concrete aisle.

"Look at this," she said with a sweep of her arm. "This is where you'll be living pretty soon. Isn't it grand?"

The Thoroughbred reached out his nose toward a stall door. Andie led him closer. It was empty.

"This exact stall might even be yours!" she told him. "I'll get a brass nameplate to put over the door that says Mr. Magic. And under your name it will say Owned by Andie Perez."

Owned by Andie Perez. Just thinking about it made shivers race down Andie's back...

ANDIE'S
RISKY BUSINESS

by Alison Hart

BULLSEYE BOOKS

Random House  New York

1

"But, Dad!" Andie Perez protested into the phone receiver. She just had to get her father to listen. "Magic *is* the right horse for me, Dad. We did so well this weekend at the inter-school horse show. Even Mrs. Caufield—she's the riding director, remember?—even she said—"

But it was no use. Andie had to hold the receiver away from her ear so she wouldn't hear all her father's annoying arguments for the zillionth time. He was so stubborn. Why couldn't he understand how much she loved Magic?

"I'll never forgive you!" she shouted into the phone and banged the receiver onto the hook. Then she spun on her stockinged feet and stomped down the hall to suite 4B, the dorm room she shared with her three roommates at Foxhall Academy, a private boarding school for girls.

When Andie slammed the door shut behind her, Mary Beth Finney, Lauren Remick, and Jinaki Williams all looked up. It was Sunday night, and study hour was over.

"So what did your dad say?" Lauren asked, her blue eyes lighting up eagerly. She sat Indian-style on her bed, combing her freshly washed blond hair. The girls had just returned from the long weekend horse show, and they were all exhausted.

Andie scowled and threw herself face first on her own bed.

"I think that means he said no," Jina replied. She was already tucked in bed, a book open on her lap. "Sorry, Andie."

"Don't feel sorry for me," Andie muttered into her pillow. "I'll find a way to own Magic, no matter what my dad says."

She peered up at her roommates. The three of them were glancing at one another with puzzled expressions.

Mary Beth turned around in her desk chair. She had been writing a letter to her family telling them all about the horse show. The two ribbons she'd won hung on her dresser mirror.

"So how are you going to do that, Andie? Steal him?"

Andie raised her brows. "Hey, good idea, Finney. I could hide him in the bathroom."

"Hide a thousand-pound animal in the bathroom! Are you kidding?" Mary Beth exclaimed. Her auburn bangs were clipped back and pimple cream dotted her forehead. Andie thought she looked like a total nerd.

"Of course I'm kidding," Andie said, annoyed. "If I steal Magic, there's no way I can hide him in the bathroom. I'd have to sneak him to another barn."

Jina frowned. "Andie, you *wouldn't*," she warned in that same superior tone Andie's father used. Jina was always so serious.

Andie sighed and rolled over on the bed. Of course she wouldn't steal Magic. But she was getting pretty desperate. She'd been trying to convince her father to buy the handsome Thoroughbred ever since she'd first seen him. Her father had consented to lease him from the school, but that wasn't enough for Andie. She wanted Magic to be *hers*.

"I can't believe how pigheaded my father is," Andie grumbled aloud.

Mary Beth giggled. "I always wondered where you got your sweet personality."

"Shut up, Finney. And what's really frustrating is that he doesn't even care how great Magic is," Andie went on, "or how much I love that horse."

"What *does* your dad care about?" Lauren asked. Standing up, she pulled her pink-flowered robe around her and went to sit beside Andie. "Maybe that will help you figure out a way to convince him to buy Magic."

"Hmm." Andie thought for a minute. Her father spent all his time being a hotshot CEO at a big company. "He loves business deals and bossing people around," she said finally. "And making money, of course."

Mary Beth snapped her fingers. "That's it! You can turn Magic into a racehorse! He'll win some races and your dad will make money."

Andie stared at Mary Beth. "You are such a noodlehead, Finney," she said. "You don't just turn a Thoroughbred into a racehorse."

"Well, at least I had an idea," Mary Beth said huffily. Abruptly pushing back her desk chair, she grabbed her shower bucket and marched into the bathroom. "And it's a lot better idea than stealing Magic," she hollered over her shoulder.

Not much better, Andie thought darkly. She stared silently at the ceiling. How was she going to buy Magic? Maybe she could write her mom a letter and send it to Spain or Greece or wherever she lived these days. She'd make it a real tearjerker.

Dear Mom,
Dad's company went broke. He's so depressed he lost all his hair. I'm so depressed I went blind. The doctors say I need an operation or I'll flunk sixth grade. Please send money.

Andie groaned to herself. Who was she kidding? Her mother didn't even care enough to send her a postcard, much less money.

Andie rolled over and pulled her pillow on top of her head. She might as well face it. No matter what Magic cost, there was no way she was ever going to get anyone to buy him for her.

"What about your allowance?" Lauren asked the next morning as she and Andie walked to breakfast. "If you saved and saved for a long time, maybe you could buy Magic yourself."

It was mid-November, and the huge oaks surrounding Foxhall's courtyard were bare. The sky was an early-morning gray, and a heavy frost had dusted the grass white. Trying to keep warm, the two girls had bundled up in jackets, scarves, and mittens.

Andie snorted. "My allowance wouldn't buy me a plastic Breyer horse. Daddy believes in investing for college. Hey!" She stopped in her tracks and spun to face Lauren. "I bet there's enough in my bank account to buy Magic!"

Lauren bit her lip. "Uh, I hate to tell you this, Andie," she said hesitantly, "but kids can't get their money out of the bank without their parents' permission."

But Andie wasn't listening. "I need to ask Caufield how much Magic would cost," she said excitedly. "Come on." Shifting her backpack to her other shoulder, Andie took off across the courtyard.

"Where are you going?" Lauren called.

"The stables," Andie called back, her breath frosty in the winter air.

"But what about breakfast?"

6

"Forget breakfast. This is too important. Are you coming?"

"Oh, I guess so." Lauren hurried to catch up.

The two of them ran under the arch that linked the stone library with Old House, Foxhall's administration building. There was so much frost on the long hill leading to the riding area that it felt almost like snow. But Andie barely noticed. All she could think about was Magic.

When they reached the horseshoe-shaped barn, Andie finally slowed down. Dorothy Germaine, Foxhall's stable manager, was walking down the outside aisleway carrying a bucket of sweetfeed. She waved at the girls, then swung around to dump feed into one of the horses' tubs.

Andie glanced toward Magic's stall. His head hung over the Dutch door as he waited eagerly for his breakfast. Clouds of frosty air blew from his nostrils. As Dorothy came closer, he let out a throaty nicker.

Andie's heart skipped a beat. Magic was so gorgeous! Dark mahogany brown with a white star.

"We'd better hurry." Lauren tugged on

7

Andie's coat sleeve. "We'll miss our first class."

The two girls sprinted across the ice-sprinkled grass to the barn office. The door was closed, but Andie could hear a radio playing inside. She knocked.

"Come in!" a voice called. Mrs. Caufield sat huddled in front of a space heater, her hands wrapped around a steaming mug of coffee. The week's riding schedule was propped in her lap.

"Isn't it a little early for your lessons?" Mrs. Caufield asked, frowning down at her watch.

"Uh." Andie hesitated in the doorway. Lauren hung back, hiding behind her.

Suddenly the director grinned and gestured for them to come in. "Shut the door, girls. It's cold outside."

Andie started to feel nervous. What if the director said Magic cost thousands of dollars? After all, Jina's horse, Superstar, had cost fifty thousand dollars. And he wasn't any prettier than Magic.

"We—I had a question about Magic," Andie said finally.

"Shoot." Mrs. Caufield eyed Andie as she took a sip of her coffee.

Andie cleared her throat. "I was wondering,

if someone was interested in buying Magic, how much would he cost?"

Mrs. Caufield raised one brow. "Why? Is your father planning on buying him?"

"Um." Andie stared down at her suede lace-up boots. "Well, he's not actually interested in buying him right *now*," she said, which wasn't a total lie.

Mrs. Caufield leaned back in the swivel chair and tossed the riding schedule on the desk. "Well, technically, because he was donated to the school, Magic is not for sale."

Andie's heart dropped to her toes.

"But," Mrs. Caufield continued, "we have made exceptions in the past, when a horse and rider were obviously right for each other."

Andie's hopes rose. "So you might—?"

"Consider it?" Mrs. Caufield finished.

Andie nodded furiously.

"Yes, I would. And because of Magic's eye problem, I'd never be able to sell Magic as sound. His price would be reasonable to the right person if she kept him here at the school."

"And how much would that price be?" Andie practically squeaked. There. She'd asked.

Mrs. Caufield shook her head. "I can't say exactly. Probably at least a thousand dollars. Why don't you have your dad call me when he's ready?"

A thousand dollars! The director's words blasted into Andie's brain. That was a lot of money, but it was cheap for a super horse like Magic. If Andie could come up with the money, Magic would finally be hers!

2

"Thanks, Mrs. Caufield," Andie heard Lauren say beside her. "We've got to get to class now." Then Andie felt someone push her toward the office door.

She blinked as the chilly air slapped her face. Suddenly she whirled and grabbed Lauren's shoulders.

"Did you hear that?" she shouted excitedly, shaking Lauren so hard that her friend's braid flew in the air. "He's only a thousand dollars! I can come up with that much money! I can buy Magic!"

"Agh!" Lauren choked out. She shoved Andie's hands from her shoulders. "Hey, I'm glad you're so happy, but you're shaking my brains loose!"

Andie frowned and tapped her lip. "Now I

just have to figure out a way to get that much money," she murmured. But where in the world would she get a thousand dollars?

"Turn to page 79 in your textbooks," Ms. Thaney told Andie's history class later that morning.

Andie opened her book, then slid a piece of paper inside the pages. On it she'd written:

WAYS TO GET MONEY
1. Earn it.
2. Borrow it.
3. Beg for it.
4. Ask for it (Christmas present?).
5. Sell stuff.
6. Steal it.
7. Counterfeit it.

All possibilities, Andie decided. Except for stealing and counterfeiting. Once she had read a book about fake money, though.

"Planning a life of crime, Ms. Perez?" a voice said behind her.

Startled, Andie snapped her book shut and jerked upright in her desk chair. Ms. Thaney was standing behind her.

"What?" Andie chirped, trying to pretend she had no idea what her teacher was talking about.

"Your list." Ms. Thaney pointed to Andie's closed book.

Andie felt her cheeks flush pink. Tossing her long wavy hair behind her shoulders, she tried to look nonchalant. All the girls in the class had turned in their seats to stare at her. Lauren was frowning, and Mary Beth was smothering a giggle with her hand.

"Oh, *that*. I was trying to figure out ways to earn enough money for, uh"—Andie racked her brains—"plane fare!" she blurted out. "My mom's in Europe, and I'm dying to see her this Christmas."

At that, Mary Beth burst into hiccuping giggles. Andie shot her a nasty look, then tipped her chin and smiled sweetly at Ms. Thaney.

Ms. Thaney pursed her lips. She wore a tailored suit and stylish wire-rimmed glasses. *Go away, you old bat*, Andie thought. But she knew Ms. Thaney wasn't really an old bat. She'd always been a pretty cool teacher— despite all the dopey stunts Andie had tried to pull in class.

Then, just as sweetly, Ms. Thaney smiled down at Andie. "Earning money for a plane ticket? What a wonderful idea. Why don't we meet this afternoon for a special session, Ms. Perez? You'll tell me exactly where your mother is living, and we'll map out all the possible plane routes."

Andie grimaced. "But I have riding this afternoon," she protested.

Ms. Thaney patted her shoulder. "I guess you'll just have to miss a few minutes, won't you?"

Andie groaned and slid down in her chair. Teachers were such a pain.

As soon as the dismissal bell rang, Andie sprang from her chair and ran for the door. Jina was right behind her.

"What was that all about?" her roommate asked when they reached the hall. Like most of the girls, Jina was dressed casually in chinos, a turtleneck, and her Foxhall blazer. Her black hair was smoothed back in a tortoiseshell hair band, and a backpack was slung over her shoulder.

Andie stopped by the doorway and sighed in exasperation. "Oh, Thaney was just giving me a hard time, as usual."

"No, I mean about money," Jina said. "Are you really going to see your mom at Christmas? I mean, if you are, that's cool. I just never hear you talk about her."

Andie snorted and shifted her backpack to her other shoulder. Someone jostled her from behind as the hall grew noisy and crowded with girls changing classes.

"Get real, Jina," she scoffed. "I don't even know where Momsie-poo is."

By now, Mary Beth, Lauren, and Tiffany Dubray were coming out of class. Tiffany was another sixth-grader, and she was doing an English project with their suite. Andie thought she was a total dork.

"So Andie's trying to figure out ways to earn money to buy Magic," Lauren was telling Tiffany and Mary Beth as they came up.

"Cool!" Mary Beth said. "How much do you need, Andie?"

"A thousand dollars," Andie replied.

Mary Beth's mouth dropped open.

"And I can do it, too, even if it takes forever," Andie said. "I just have to figure out a way."

"I'll help," Jina offered. "I can contribute some of my baby-sitting money. Whitney's mom always pays me way too much."

"And I'll give you some of my allowance," Lauren chimed in.

Andie smiled. It was nice of her two room-mates to offer, but..."Thanks, guys. That'll help. It won't add up to much, though. I need to think of something *big*."

"*Really* big," Mary Beth said.

Andie slipped her list from her book. "Look, I wrote down seven possible ways to get money."

The girls gathered around Andie, peering at the list. Pointing to number six, Tiffany snick-ered. "I can picture you robbing a bank, Andie."

"Oh, shut up, Dubray." Andie glanced over at the blond girl. Tiffany was always dressed up. But today she'd outdone herself. She wore a red sequin-dotted sweater over green velour leggings. "Gee, Tiff, did anyone tell you you looked like a Christmas tree?"

Tiffany bristled. "No," she snapped. Spin-ning around, she marched down the hall, her nose in the air.

"Andie!" Lauren scolded. "Why are you always so mean to poor Tiffany?"

Andie ignored her roommate. She was too busy thinking.

16

"Well, I've got to get to my next class," Jina said finally.

"Me too," Lauren added. The two of them said good-bye and disappeared down the hall.

Slowly, Andie headed in the other direction, absorbed in moneymaking possibilities. She could look up the address on the last postcard her mom had sent and write that letter begging for money.

She could sell her old riding boots, too. And for Christmas she'd ask for money instead of gifts. That would be a start. But she still needed something *big*.

"A thousand dollars," Mary Beth muttered beside her. She was shaking her head in disbelief. "If you have to make that much money, you'd better get a job," she added, frowning seriously.

A job!

Andie stopped dead in her tracks. Why hadn't she thought of that?

"Thanks, roomie!" Andie cried, giving Mary Beth a quick hug. "You just gave me a brilliant idea! With a job, I should be able to earn enough money to buy Magic in a couple of weeks!"

3

"I'm glad to see you and Magic finally made it to your lesson, Ms. Perez," Mrs. Caufield said when Andie jogged beside Magic into the indoor ring. The director was bundled in a heavy quilted coat, a muffler around her neck.

"Ms. Thaney kept me after class," Andie explained quickly as she led Magic over to the mounting block. Gathering her reins, she stuck her left toe into the stirrup and swung into the saddle. Even though she wore warm gloves, her fingers were already stiff with cold.

Eager to get going, Magic strode off. Andie halted him and made him back up. Mary Beth and two other beginning riders, Heidi Olsen and Shandra Thomas, were already mounted and waiting patiently. They watched in silence as Andie tried to get Magic to stand still long enough to slip her right toe in the stirrup.

"Having trouble?" Mary Beth teased when Magic danced past her and Dangerous Dan, the huge, dead-quiet school horse she rode.

Andie stuck her tongue out at her roommate. It was bad enough that she had to ride with the baby beginners today. But if Magic acted up the whole lesson, she'd really be embarrassed.

The young Thoroughbred was full of himself this afternoon. The ground had frozen, so Dorothy hadn't turned him out in the pasture. Andie usually longed him before she rode, but this afternoon, she'd been too late.

"Trot him in small circles at the end of the ring," Mrs. Caufield called. "When he's warmed up and settled, he can join the others for our canter lesson."

Canter lesson? Andie's stomach lurched. She'd been cantering horses since she was seven, but this would be the first time she'd cantered Magic. Ever since he'd had his eye operation, he'd improved steadily. But she could never forget the time he'd thrown Katherine Parks, the dressage instructor. Posting slowly, her seat deep, Andie tried to relax so Magic would relax, too. He tugged on the reins, trying to duck his head and crow-hop. Andie squeezed her legs against his sides, pushing him forward and into a tighter circle. Slowly, his stride lengthened and the tension left his neck and back.

Fifteen minutes later, they trotted back to the group. Everyone was listening to Mrs. Caufield.

"The canter is a three-beat gait," the director was saying. "It has more of a rocking motion than the trot, so you need to sit down in the saddle and let your body move easily with your horse."

Andie halted Magic next to Dan and glanced over at Mary Beth. Her roommate was gritting her teeth. Andie knew that this was Mary Beth's first time cantering—ever. Poor Finney was probably scared to death.

"Today we're not going to worry about leads, which I'll explain later," Mrs. Caufield continued as she walked back and forth. "You'll trot to the end of the arena, sit a trot at the first corner, then squeeze with your outside leg, signaling your horse to canter."

A sharp pang of fear stabbed Andie. *But what if your horse tries to buck you off?*

"Canter the length of the arena," Mrs. Caufield went on. "Keep contact with your rein, but be careful not to pull on your horse's mouth."

Hesitantly, Andie raised her hand. "Um, what if—" she began.

Mary Beth, Heidi, and Shandra turned to look at her. Gulping, Andie glanced down at her fingers clenched on the rein.

She *couldn't* ask Caufield what to do if Magic bucked or ran away. If she did, the other riders would think she was a scared baby beginner—just like them.

"Never mind," Andie mumbled.

Mrs. Caufield nodded toward Heidi. She was mounted on Windsor, a big-boned warm-blood who was almost twenty years old. "Heidi will go first," the director said. "All she'll need to do is be clear with her aids, since Windsor likes to canter. And what will those aids be, Mary Beth?"

"Sit deep and squeeze with your outside leg," Mary Beth answered, her voice a high croak.

At least I'm not the only one who's nervous, Andie thought.

She watched Heidi trot Windsor to the far end of the arena. At the first corner, Heidi collected him to a sitting trot, then asked him to canter at the second corner. The big bay went smoothly down the side. Heidi grinned and bounced the whole way.

"She makes it look so easy," Mary Beth said out of the side of her mouth.

"Very nice, Heidi," Mrs. Caufield called. "Mary Beth, you're next."

Mary Beth jerked upright in the saddle. "Me?" she squeaked.

Mrs. Caufield laughed. "Yes, you. Now, since Dan's a little lazy, you need to carry your crop in your outside hand. Give him little leg squeezes to wake him up, then nudge him hard with that outside leg. If he ignores you, tap him behind the girth with the crop."

Mary Beth nodded grimly as Dan began walking across the arena. When they reached the first corner, she sat to the trot. Andie grimaced as she watched her roommate jiggle and flop in the saddle.

Poor Mary Beth, she thought.

"Remember, wake Dan up with your leg, then signal him to canter," Mrs. Caufield called.

Mary Beth pressed her legs hard against Dan's sides. The big horse ignored her and continued to trot steadily down the side. Holding the rein in her inside hand, Mary Beth reached around with the crop. Before she could even tap him, Dan suddenly broke into a slow canter.

Startled, Mary Beth hit the saddle hard, and her crop flew through the air. Grabbing Dan's mane, she hung on tight.

At the end of the arena, Dan abruptly halted. Mary Beth lurched forward, catching herself on his neck. Her gasp of relief was so loud that everyone laughed.

"Uh, good, Mary Beth," Mrs. Caufield said, hesitating only slightly. "Next time, we'll work on a smoother depart. Andie, your turn."

Andie stopped laughing. *This is it*, she thought.

She gathered her reins, and Magic strode eagerly to the far end of the arena. She could feel the beginners watching behind her. Then she saw three other girls, Foxhall seniors, hanging around the open arena door. She knew one of them, Melanie Harden, who was president of the Horse Masters Club.

Andie gulped. The three girls were staring at her and pointing. *What are you jerks looking at?* she wanted to yell. She just knew they wanted to see her get bucked off.

"We're waiting, Andie!" Mrs. Caufield called. "If Magic seems too eager or gets playful, keep contact with the reins and drive him forward with your seat. A horse can't buck when he's moving ahead with energy. And remember, use voice commands."

Andie nodded, then took a deep breath. Magic broke into a fast trot. Andie circled him, settled him, and at the first corner, sat deep. The Thoroughbred broke into a canter as soon as she touched him with her outside heel and commanded, "Canter."

Smoothly, softly, and on the correct lead, Magic cantered down the side. Andie felt almost as though she were flying.

"Keep going around the entire arena," Mrs. Caufield instructed.

When they finally slowed to a walk, Andie threw her arms around Magic's neck. "You are so wonderful!" she cried.

Heidi, Shandra, and Mary Beth let out cheers, and even Mrs. Caufield said, "Very nice, Andie."

Then she heard slow, rhythmic clapping. Straightening, Andie glanced over at the three seniors. Melanie Harden was clapping as she checked Andie out with narrowed eyes.

Andie frowned. *What is going on?* she wondered. Melanie Harden didn't even know her. Why the sudden interest?

Then it dawned on her. Melanie wasn't looking at her. She was watching *Magic*.

But why?

Twenty minutes later, Mrs. Caufield dismissed the girls from their lesson. Still mounted, Andie walked Magic around, slowly cooling him off. A few minutes later, she saw Melanie stroll into the center of the ring to talk to the riding director. Curious, Andie circled Magic closer.

"Yes, Magic *is* a nice horse. Andie's leasing him this semester," she heard Mrs. Caufield say as the two started walking toward the exit. "But her lease will be up in December, so we'll see."

Andie's breath caught in her throat. *See what?* she thought wildly.

But when Melanie stopped by the door and turned to study Magic one last time, Andie knew what the senior wanted.

She wanted Magic.

Quickly, Andie steered the Thoroughbred away from Melanie's prying gaze. Tears filled her eyes and she bit her lip hard.

She couldn't blame Melanie for wanting Magic. He was special, and soon every rider at Foxhall would know it. That meant she had to buy him before the semester was up.

She had to get that money—fast!

4

"So, Jina, how much money do you make baby-sitting?" Andie asked her roommate that night. She was lying flat on her back on her bed, her legs propped against the wall.

Jina looked up from her math homework. "Mrs. Chambers gives me five dollars an hour."

"Five dollars an hour!" Mary Beth and Lauren chorused from the floor. They were rereading the play based on *Black Beauty* that they'd written for their English project.

"I've never been paid five dollars an hour in my life," Mary Beth sputtered.

"That's because you live in hicky old Cedarville," Andie said. "Probably even the mayor doesn't get five dollars an hour."

"I've never gotten that much, either," Lauren admitted.

"Well, I'll be such a *great* baby-sitter, everybody will want to pay me seven dollars," Andie said. She wrote the amount in the notebook that rested against her upraised legs.

At that, Mary Beth, Lauren, and Jina burst out laughing.

"Maybe they'll pay you that much *not* to baby-sit," Lauren teased.

Andie just nodded. "That's fine, too. Now let's see. One thousand divided by seven dollars equals..." Pausing, she quickly computed the problem on her paper. "Oh, great," she grumbled. "I'd have to baby-sit about a hundred and forty-three hours to make a thousand dollars!"

She groaned and crumpled up her paper. "I need the money by the end of December. You should have seen how Melanie Harden was drooling over Magic."

Mary Beth stood up and stretched. "I think you're imagining things," she said, reaching for the soda she'd set on her desk. "Melanie was just watching the lesson."

"How would you know?" Andie shot back. "You were too busy flopping around on Dan."

Mary Beth flushed so red that her freckles disappeared. "You don't have to rub it in,

Andie. I know I stunk." She yanked open the door of the wardrobe that separated her and Lauren's beds.

"That was mean, Andie," Lauren said in a low voice. "Today was Mary Beth's first time cantering. I bet you weren't so perfect your first time, either."

Andie bit her lip. Lauren was right. As usual, she was taking out her frustrations on her roommates.

"Sorry, Mary Beth," she said. "You didn't do so bad. I'm just mad about everything. I'm never going to get enough money to buy Magic."

"Not baby-sitting," Jina agreed. She shut her math notebook and leaned back in her desk chair. "You'll have to think of a different job. One that pays more."

Andie sighed "Who's going to hire a kid?"

"Oh, rats," Mary Beth grumbled. Her head was inside the open wardrobe. "I can't believe all my pajamas are dirty."

"I'd lend you one of my nighties, but I didn't have time to do laundry this weekend, either," Lauren said.

"Dirty laundry, yuck." Jina shook her head. "I'd rather muck out stalls for a week."

Andie abruptly sat up and snapped her fingers. "That's it!" she cried. "That's who'll hire a kid—other kids!"

"Huh?" Jina, Mary Beth, and Lauren stared at her with puzzled expressions.

"I bet lots of Foxhall students would pay me to do their laundry," Andie said excitedly.

"Hey, that's a great idea," Lauren said. She went over and sat next to Andie. "I bet there are tons of chores you could do. Especially for some of those lazy, stuck-up juniors and seniors—like my sister."

Mary Beth pulled a wadded-up nightshirt from the wardrobe and held it up. "Pee-yu. This thing stinks. *I'd* pay you to do my laundry, Andie, if I had enough money."

"I'll just have to find girls who are rich *and* lazy," Andie said. Springing off the bed, she paced across the suite. "If I did chores for other students, I could earn money every day. Not just on Saturdays like if I baby-sat."

Whirling around, Andie dove for the notebook and pencil she'd left on the bed. "Hmm. There are about twenty-five days left till the semester's over," she muttered as she jotted down the number. "Divide that into a thousand dollars and..." A minute later, she waved

30

the paper excitedly. "I'd only have to make forty dollars a day! And if I got some money for Christmas, plus allowance and other stuff, it means—"

She paused, gazing at her roommates in shock. All three stared back at her.

"What does it mean?" Mary Beth prompted. She was still clutching her wrinkled nightie.

Andie inhaled sharply. "I could make all the money by the end of the semester!"

Lauren squealed in excitement. "That's so cool."

"I don't know." Jina shook her head doubtfully. "Forty dollars a day is a lot of chores. When are you going to find the time?"

Lauren leaped off the bed. "I've got it!" she exclaimed. "If Jina, Mary Beth, and I help, you could really make the money fast. Each of us would only have to earn ten dollars a day!"

Andie raised her brows. "You guys would do that?"

Lauren looked hesitantly at Jina and Mary Beth. Jina spun in her chair and whipped open her math notebook. Just as fast, Mary Beth began to root busily through the wardrobe again.

"Well, *I'd* help," Lauren said.

"I just can't find anything clean," Mary Beth mumbled to herself.

Lauren tapped her foot and waited.

"What?" Mary Beth asked, turning around.

"You know what," Lauren told her.

Exhaling loudly, Mary Beth threw up her hands. "Oh, all right. I'll help, too. Though with all the homework we get, I don't know when I'll find the time."

"What about you, Jina?" Lauren asked sweetly.

Without turning, Jina nodded reluctantly. "But only until the semester's over."

"Wow!" Andie burst out. Her roommates were really going to help her! "Thanks, guys!" Grabbing Mary Beth, then Lauren, by their elbows, she spun them around until all three of them were breathless with laughter.

"You'll see," Andie gasped finally, falling back on her bed. "It'll be easy. I bet we'll make a thousand dollars by the end of the month!"

5

"Make other kids' beds?" Mary Beth asked doubtfully. "We barely have time to make our own in the mornings."

The four roommates were walking slowly up the hill to the stables for their Tuesday afternoon lessons. The ground was frozen hard, and dark clouds rolled across the sky.

"We can do it," Andie said. As she walked, she scribbled furiously in the notebook she was carrying. "We'll charge fifty cents a bed. I bet dozens of girls will hire us."

"We'll have to set our alarms half an hour early," Lauren suggested. Turning toward Mary Beth, she pulled her wool scarf tighter around her neck. "It'll only be for a month."

"I can handle that." Jina peered over Andie's arm at the notebook. A brisk wind whipped down the hill, fluttering the pages. "What else is on that list?"

The girls were dressed in their riding clothes. Andie wore a jacket over her sweatshirt, long underwear under her breeches, two pairs of socks, thick gloves, a scarf, and earmuffs under her helmet. Still, the winter wind went right through her.

Smoothing the rustling notebook pages, Andie read out loud:

"1. Vacuum/dust room—five dollars.
2. Laundry—two dollars a load, plus expenses.
3. Deliver snacks/soda—fifty cents a trip.
4. Make beds—fifty cents a bed or three dollars a week.
5. Clean bathroom—five dollars."

"Ugh. Sounds like a lot of work," Mary Beth complained when Andie finished.

"You are such a wimp, Finney," Andie said, rolling her eyes.

Mary Beth pressed her lips together. "Well, couldn't there be some fun chores?"

"Like what?"

Mary Beth thought for a moment. "More stuff like selling my mom's cookies."

Andie nodded. "Yeah. It's a good thing we called her last night. That selling snacks idea you had was a great one, Finney." Andie whacked her on the back.

"What about doing some horse stuff?" Jina suggested. "That's fun—kind of."

"Yeah!" Lauren brightened. "We could groom other people's horses, pull manes—"

"Clean tack and boots," Jina chimed in.

"Yes! Yes! Yes!" Grinning happily, Andie scribbled everything down in the notebook. "You guys are brilliant. I love you!" Holding out her arms as if to hug them, she made kissing noises in the air.

"Gross!" Lauren, Jina, and Mary Beth chorused. They dodged Andie's embrace, then raced giggling up the hill to the barn.

"Change of plans, girls!" Dorothy Germaine announced when the four of them barreled into the tack room. The stable manager was bundled up in a thick coat and insulated rubber boots that made her look even wider than usual.

Andie screeched to a halt so fast that Lauren, Jina, and Mary Beth plowed into her.

"We're not riding?" she asked, not bothering to keep the disappointment out of her voice.

"Too windy and cold. Everybody's grooming their horses and checking their water. In half an hour, we'll meet in Mrs. Caufield's office for a lecture and slide show."

Andie groaned. "I hope it's not about her summer vacation," she whispered to Jina.

"I heard that," Dorothy said gruffly. "Actually, it's all about *my* summer vacation. Now hustle and take care of your horses, then head straight to the office."

Grabbing Magic's grooming kit and halter, Andie hurried to his stall. Lauren headed in the opposite direction to groom her school horse, Whisper, and Mary Beth cut across the courtyard to take care of Dan. Jina left for the new barn, which housed the horses owned by Foxhall students.

When Andie reached Magic's stall, she opened the top half of the Dutch door. A gust of wind whistled down the outside aisle, snatching the door from her hands. It banged loudly against the wall. Snorting, Magic jumped to the other side of his stall.

"It's just me, buddy," Andie crooned soothingly. She opened the bottom half of the door and walked into his stall.

Ears rotating like radar antennas, Magic

greeted her with a low nicker. Andie scratched his forehead, a huge bubble of happiness swelling in her chest.

Soon Magic would be hers! She'd never had a pet of her own. Not even a stupid fish. "You're not responsible enough," her mother had always said, no matter what animal Andie begged for. "The housekeeper will end up taking care of it." *And you should know, Momsie*, Andie thought bitterly. *The housekeeper took care of me when you left.*

Andie hugged Magic's neck. "I'll always take good care of *you*," she vowed as she slipped the halter over his muzzle. "And when you're mine, I can board you in the new barn with Superstar instead of this drafty old place. How's that sound?"

Andie buckled the halter and snapped on a lead line. Then she began to undo all the straps on Magic's quilted blanket. It was dull green with dingy white straps. Though it had been washed many times, stubborn manure stains spotted the sides.

"I'll buy you a new blanket, too. It won't have straps that rub, and it'll be a beautiful, bright blue."

Stepping forward, Magic poked his head

over the stall's bottom door. His forelock blew in the sharp wind as he raised his head and nickered. An answering whinny came from across the courtyard. Tossing his head, Magic pawed the straw.

Andie laughed. "I know. You want to go out and play. Hey, how about if I buy you *two* new blankets? One for the barn and one for turnout. Then you can run around outside even on the coldest days. You'll be the best-dressed horse at Foxhall."

Andie pulled off the blanket and folded it in half. Then she backed Magic away from the door and carried the blanket outside, where she gave it several good shakes. "Achoo!" Dust flew everywhere.

When Andie was done, she hung the blanket over the door, then went back in the stall to groom Magic. Every day, she brushed him until he gleamed. There was no way some stupid grown-up could ever accuse her of not taking care of Magic.

"Hi. You're Andie, right?"

Startled, Andie spun around. Melanie Harden was leaning on the stall door. A red stocking cap covered most of her shiny black hair.

"Yeah, that's me," Andie answered shortly. Avoiding the older girl's gaze, she dropped the currycomb into the grooming kit and plucked out a dandy brush.

"Magic looks great," Melanie said, holding out her hand to him, palm up.

Curious, the big horse stretched his neck to sniff her fingers.

Don't touch him, Andie wanted to snap.

But she kept her mouth shut. What did Ms. Big Shot President of the Horse Masters Club want?

"Can I help you with something?" Andie asked, forcing herself to be polite. With one eye on Melanie, she continued to brush Magic.

The dark-haired girl was tall and slender, with big brown eyes, fluttery lashes, creamy-white skin, and rosebud lips.

Kind of pretty, Andie had to admit, *if you like Barbie dolls.*

"Yeah, you can help me," Melanie replied. "Tell me some stuff about Mr. Magic here."

"Why?" Andie asked, brushing faster.

"Well, I'm graduating this year, and my parents have promised to buy me a horse."

Andie's arm froze in mid-stroke. Her breath

caught in her throat. "Oh? And you are interested in Magic?" she finally choked out.

Melanie nodded. "Definitely. I'm applying to colleges with major riding programs, so I'll be taking my new horse with me."

Andie gulped hard. *Stay calm, Perez,* she told herself. *You can handle this.*

"Well, that sounds great." Andie started to brush again. "Magic's a really nice horse. It's just too bad about..." Her voice trailed off.

"Too bad about what?"

Andie sighed deeply. "It's too bad about his *eye*." She shook her head as if the situation was hopeless.

Melanie nodded. "I know about the operation. But Mrs. Caufield said it was very successful."

"Yeah. But the veterinarian, Dr. Holden, said just the slightest trauma and rip-p-p!" She jerked her hands dramatically. "That retina could become detached again. Maybe permanently this time."

"Really?" Melanie frowned in disappointment. "That's too bad. Such a nice horse, too. I bet he had a lot of potential."

Turning away, Andie bit back a grin. *Gotcha!* she thought.

Then she realized Melanie was watching her closely. "You know, Andie, I think you're trying to pull a fast one on me," the older girl said, her voice low. "I've been warned about you. You've got quite a reputation for a sixth-grader."

Andie bristled, her fingers clenching tightly around the brush. Then she took a deep breath, willing herself to be cool. She had to convince Melanie that Magic wasn't the right horse for her.

"Well, I don't care what your friends said," she said, her voice oozing with innocence. "I'm telling you the truth." *Kind of*, she added silently.

"Oh, yeah? Well, if you're not, you'll be sorry. Mrs. Caufield said your lease is up in December. So just remember—he's not *yours*." Melanie shot Andie a determined look. "And if I like him enough, he just might be *mine!*"

"No way!" Andie glared at Melanie. "Magic will never be yours!"

The older girl smiled coolly, then turned and walked away.

Say something! Andie told herself frantically. *Tell her you're going to buy Magic!*

Rushing to the stall door, she leaned over and peered across the courtyard. She could just see Melanie's back as she disappeared into the stable office.

"Magic may not be mine yet!" Andie hollered after her. "But he will be—and soon! So you can't have him, Miss Big Shot! *You can't have him!*"

The office door shut. The icy wind burned Andie's cheeks. Had Melanie heard her?

A soft muzzle pressed against Andie's back. Tears pricked her eyes. Turning, she wrapped her arms around Magic's neck, breathing in his warmth.

Not fair, she sobbed into his neck. *It's just not fair!*

Melanie Harden's father was going to buy his daughter a horse. Why wouldn't Andie's father buy Magic for her?

Straightening, Andie brushed the tears off her cheeks.

Well, she didn't care what Melanie and her stupid father did. And she didn't care what her own pigheaded father did. She was going to buy Magic herself.

That slimy Melanie wasn't going to get Magic.

Ever.

"Protecting horses against winter weather is very important," Mrs. Caufield was saying when Andie quietly entered the heated office.

About twenty girls were sprawled everywhere around the room. Andie found a seat on the floor next to Lauren, who was leaning against Mrs. Caufield's desk. Mary Beth and

Jina were on the other side of the office, squeezed between some girls sitting on a row of tack boxes.

"Winter care begins in the fall with worming and a checkup," the director said. "If horses are in good physical shape, they can easily withstand below-freezing temperatures."

Slowly, Mrs. Caufield walked around the packed room, passing out work sheets. "Horses have two defenses against the cold," she continued, "long coat hair and a layer of fat under the skin that insulates…"

Automatically, Andie tuned Mrs. Caufield out. It wasn't that she didn't care. She was just too worried.

"Andie?" Mrs. Caufield stopped in front of the desk. When Andie looked up, the director handed her a work sheet. WINTER CARE FOR YOUR HORSE was written on the top. "Are you with us this afternoon?" she asked.

Looking down at her boots, Andie nodded. She couldn't meet the riding director's eyes. If Caufield was telling Melanie all about Magic, then she obviously wasn't on Andie's side.

"Uh-oh. Looks like this stuff will be Friday's pop quiz," Lauren whispered to Andie as Mrs. Caufield walked away.

"Too often, the importance of water in cold weather is overlooked," the director continued. "In the pasture we have electric heaters in the tanks, and in the new barn the automatic waterers won't freeze. But here in the old barn, we have to constantly monitor the buckets. If the horse drinks too little water, there's a chance of an impacted intestine and colic."

Lauren raised her hand and waved it vigorously.

"Yes, Lauren?"

"If the horses don't mind the cold, why can't we ride today?"

"Yeah, why can't we ride?" other girls' voices echoed around the room.

Mrs. Caufield glanced at the students. "Does anyone want to answer Lauren's question?"

"I will," a voice called from the corner.

Andie craned her neck, trying to see around the desk. A groan escaped her lips when she saw who had volunteered.

Melanie.

"Who is it?" Lauren asked in a low voice.

"Melanie Harden," Andie replied. "That witch."

Lauren scrunched her brows as she studied

the older girl. "I think she's pretty."

"You would." Andie snorted as she hunched back against the desk.

"Andie? Are you listening to Melanie's answer?" Mrs. Caufield asked.

Andie snapped her chin up. "Oh, yes!" she said with fake enthusiasm. "I'm soaking up every word."

"Even though the school horses are blanketed to keep their hair short, they still get hot and sweaty during lessons," Melanie explained. "And if a hot horse isn't cooled down properly, it can get chills or pneumonia."

"Show-off," Andie muttered. Loosening her wool scarf, she scowled down at the floor.

"Thank you, Melanie." Mrs. Caufield smiled warmly. "All you girls have been taught how to cool down a horse, but in windy weather like this, it's very difficult and time-consuming, and the chance of a chill increases. Now, let me finish going over this work sheet, then Dorothy has a treat for you."

Andie glanced at the slide projector set up in the middle of the room. "And I bet it's called 'My Boring Summer,'" she said to Lauren in a low voice.

Lauren giggled. "Actually, that might be

pretty cool. Dorothy told me she worked at a ranch out west for a few weeks and went on a cattle drive." For a moment she studied Andie. "So, why don't you like Melanie?" she asked finally.

Andie swung her gaze back to the raven-haired girl. "'Cause she thinks she's so hot. And because she wants Magic."

Lauren leaned closer. "She wants Magic?"

Andie nodded. "Yeah. Only she's not going to get him," she declared, glowering at Melanie. "Because tonight, we're going to start our business. And when I get a hundred dollars, I'm putting a deposit on Magic. Then he'll be mine for sure."

"So you want us to clean your room this Friday?" Andie repeated, writing hurriedly in her notebook. It was Wednesday afternoon, and she was standing in the doorway of suite 2E. Celina Glenn, a senior who roomed in the suite, nodded.

"And make our beds *every* morning," Celina said. She reached into her jeans pocket and pulled out a ten-dollar bill. "This is for this morning. Tell Mary Beth and Lauren they can keep the change. The bathroom's never been cleaner."

Andie nodded vigorously as she jotted down the amount. "Right." She took the money and stuffed it in the fanny pack around her waist, grinning to herself. This was the part she loved best. Getting paid.

"We'll see you tomorrow morning then," Andie said. "Oh, by the way. How about our snack service? We offer homemade cookies, chips, and popcorn. Guaranteed to be fresher than the ones in the machine."

"Hmm." Celina thought for a moment. "Sounds good. Why don't you come by this evening after study hall? My roommate and I are usually starved by then."

Andie smiled. Anything to please the customer.

When Celina shut the door, Andie punched the air with her fist. "Yes!"

She rushed upstairs, taking the steps two at a time. When she burst into suite 4B, she almost ran over Jina and Mary Beth, who were sitting on the floor. Several huge bowls of popcorn and potato chips and a box of cookies were in front of them.

"It's about time you got here," Mary Beth said, furiously scooping popcorn into a small plastic bag. "We need help. Riding starts in twenty minutes."

Andie glanced around the suite. "Why isn't Lauren helping?"

"She had to talk to her math teacher," Jina said. She was counting out potato chips. "She's

49

having trouble with fractions again."

Andie dropped to her knees and began to stuff cookies in a bag. "I can't believe how many girls want us to do chores for them," she said. "Those flyers we printed really did the trick. I finally discovered something useful to do with a computer."

"Did you look at the messages on our memo board?" Jina asked, without looking up.

"No."

"There are a whole bunch of them. All from girls wanting us to do laundry or clean."

"All right!" Andie whooped. She filled a second bag, then leaned back on her heels. "We can finish bagging snacks tonight and take them around after study hall. From the response I've been getting, I'd say everyone in the dorm is going to want to buy some." She smiled at Mary Beth. "Especially those cookies your mom sent."

Mary Beth grunted as she twisted a tie around a bag. "Those packs of microwave popcorn Jina's mom sent us are great, too. Each pack made a lot."

"So far, we've got twenty-one bags of popcorn," Jina counted. "It took forever to pop it all. I was using the microwave in the common room for ages, and everyone was pretty mad at me for tying it up. We also have fifteen bags of chips, and twelve bags of cookies— three cookies to a bag."

"That's not going to last very long." Andie frowned. "Do you think your mom would make more cookies for us, Mary Beth?"

Mary Beth shrugged. "Sure. But I don't know about the overnight postage. That's pretty expensive."

Jina stood up and stretched. "Tell her it's for a worthy cause." She looked up at her hands. "Yuck. I'm covered with salt and grease," she said, and headed for the bathroom.

Mary Beth and Andie piled the filled bags onto Andie's bed. Then they hurried to find their riding clothes.

Dropping down on a chair, Andie pulled on two pairs of socks. "We'd better hurry. You're scheduled to groom Snowman this afternoon," she told Mary Beth.

"Whose horse is that?" Mary Beth asked, opening her bottom drawer.

"Stacey Meadow's. He's that big gray gelding that's stabled in the new barn."

Abruptly, Mary Beth straightened. Her eyes

were wide with horror. "You mean that horse who tries to bite you when you walk by?"

Andie tugged on her high black rubber boots. "Yup, that's the one. But don't worry. He's a pussycat."

"Then he's the meanest pussycat I've ever seen," Mary Beth grumbled as she yanked her corduroy coat off the hanger.

"Jina!" Andie called into the bathroom. "Ashley Stewart wants you to clean her tack!"

"What?" Jina appeared in the open doorway, her hands dripping wet.

"Clean her tack. Before the weekend."

Jina's jaw dropped. "Why me? Did you tell her I'd do it? You know I don't like that girl." Before Jina's horse, Superstar, had been injured, Jina and Ashley had been rivals at many shows.

Andie stood up and reached for her jacket. "Well, she asked for you. She said you were the only one who could do a good job."

"Oh, sure," Jina sputtered. "She just wants to rub my nose in the fact that she's showing this weekend and I'm not." Wiping her hands on her pants, she spun around and went back into the bathroom.

Andie checked her watch. "I wish Lauren

would hurry up. She's supposed to clean T.L. for Missy."

"She should be here any minute." Mary Beth picked up her riding helmet. "Well, I'd better get to the barn if I'm grooming Dan and Snowman." She hesitated. "Are you sure Snowman's a pussycat?"

"Positive," Andie assured her. "But don't turn your back on him, just to be safe."

Mary Beth rolled her eyes. "Great."

Lauren suddenly burst into the suite, shoving the door so hard it smacked into the wall. Mary Beth jumped back just in time.

"Gotta hurry!" Lauren gasped, out of breath. Throwing her books and backpack on her bed, she ran to her dresser drawer.

"You'd better hurry, all right," Mary Beth warned. "Andie's cracking the whip." With a wave good-bye, she shut the door behind her.

"You only have to groom T.L.," Andie told Lauren. "It shouldn't take that long."

"I barely have time to do Whisper," Lauren complained as she yanked her breeches right over her leggings.

Just then Jina came out of the bathroom. She wore blue Polar Fleece schooling pants and a matching vest.

"Wow, what a neat outfit!" Lauren said. "Where'd you get it?"

Jina dropped her gaze. Her mom was always buying her expensive clothes, and Andie knew it sometimes embarrassed her.

"My mom sent it...So what did Mrs. Jacquin say?"

Lauren sighed. "My math grades aren't so hot. She suggested we try another tutor."

"Not *Ashley*, I hope." Andie zipped her jacket and picked up her helmet.

"No, not Ashley."

Jina sighed. "She'll be too busy bossing me around."

Lauren gave Andie an accusing look.

"Hey." Andie held up a hand in defense. "It wasn't my idea. Besides, I'm charging snotty old Ashley big bucks. Are you guys ready?" She headed to the door.

"Almost." Jina pulled her black boots from under her bed, and Lauren disappeared into the bathroom.

Andie checked the messages on the memo board that hung on the outside of the suite door. There were five more requests. She wrote the girls' names and suite numbers down in her notebook.

So far, they had booked over twenty jobs. And they'd only passed flyers out in their own dorm. Maybe they could also hand them out in Mill Hall. That way, they could double the number of jobs. And double the money, too!

Clutching her helmet under her arm, Andie danced into the hall. Things couldn't be going better. Andie Perez, Inc., was off to a flying start!

Grinning happily, Andie spun in a circle. Jina dashed from the suite, crashing into her. Andie's notebook fluttered to the floor and her helmet crashed to her feet.

"Hey, watch out!"

"Sorry." Jina picked up the helmet and thrust it at Andie. Then she ran down the hall, calling over her shoulder, "If I'm going to clean Ashley's tack, I have to get moving. Tomorrow's my day to ride Applejacks at Middlefield. I won't have time then."

Andie frowned. "You mean you won't be here to do chores on Thursday afternoons?" she muttered.

"I've got to get out of here, too," Lauren said, rushing past Andie, "since I've got *two* horses to groom."

Quickly, Andie retrieved her notebook from the floor. Then she ran after her roommates.

"I guess I better make a schedule for us," Andie said as the three girls clomped down the steps in their boots.

"Good idea," Jina replied. She reached the ground floor first, pushing through the heavy exit door. A blast of cold air rushed into the dorm.

Andie tucked her helmet under her arm and pulled on a striped stocking cap. "I'll post the schedule on our memo board. Then everyone—even our clients—will know who's doing what and when."

Jina gave her a funny look. "Our *clients*?"

Andie shrugged. "Sure. What else would we call them?"

Lauren giggled as the girls ran up the hill. "Let's call them our *masters*. Because I'm beginning to feel like a slave!"

"Good job, Andie," Mrs. Caufield called across the outdoor ring. "Magic looked a little more balanced at the canter today. We'll work on leads tomorrow."

Andie nodded. Her breath came in cloudy bursts as she told Magic to walk. He jogged several steps, then slowed. Andie reached down and gave him several solid pats on the neck. "You liked that, huh?"

The Thoroughbred tugged on the reins, his stride lengthening. Andie knew he was feeling good this crisp, sunny afternoon. She'd had to keep a taut rein and ride lots of circles. But even after an hour lesson, he was ready for more.

"Soon," she told him. "Soon, we'll be able to go on trail rides and canter in the fields. Then we'll really have fun."

"All right, beginners, listen up." Mrs. Caufield turned her attention to Mary Beth, Heidi, and Shandra. "You, too, Andie."

Andie smiled gratefully as she rode Magic toward the others. She didn't mind riding with the baby beginners as long as everyone knew she wasn't one.

"This is the coldest day we've worked," the director said, "so the job of putting away your horses will take a little longer. Walk them in the ring for at least ten minutes to let their muscles cool gradually. Then dismount. When you get back to the barn, rub your horse down, cover him with a sweat sheet, and continue walking. I want to check all your mounts before you blanket them for the night."

"Ugh," Mary Beth said to Andie. She'd halted Dan beside Magic. "That will take forever. And I haven't groomed Snowman yet."

Andie raised her brows. "Why not?"

"Because I had to do Dan first," Mary Beth said. "He was in the pasture all day and must have rolled in every pile of frozen manure."

"Well, you'd better hurry and groom Snowman before dinner or we won't get paid."

Mary Beth stiffened in the saddle. "You could help me, you know."

"I would love to," Andie said quickly. "But I've got a ton to do, too. I've got to meet with three other riders who want tack cleaned, check on Jina, then see if Lauren groomed T.L."

"Oh, gee, gosh, golly. I guess you *are* busy," Mary Beth huffed. Kicking Dan abruptly, she steered him in the other direction.

What's her problem? Andie wondered. Then she spotted Lauren riding Whisper up the hill from the indoor arena. Here was her chance to check and see if Lauren had finished T.L.

"Yeah, I brushed him, but I was late for my lesson with Katherine," Lauren said, halting Whisper by the gate. "And she was mad."

Magic stuck his nose over the fence and tried to sniff the chestnut mare. Before Andie could turn him away, Whisper pinned her ears and squealed.

"So don't do that to me again, Andie," Lauren said shortly, backing Whisper up. "It's just too hard to fit in extra work before riding."

Andie was surprised by her roommate's tone. She was usually so bubbly and helpful. Maybe Mary Beth's grumpy mood had rubbed off on her.

When Magic's neck felt cool, Andie dismounted and led him to the barn. The courtyard was filled with girls untacking horses. The sun was starting to set, and the air was growing colder.

Andie unsaddled Magic and put on his halter. To finish cooling him off, she rubbed away sweat marks with a damp sponge. Then she briskly towel-dried him. Finally, she draped a sweat sheet over his back and rump.

"That's one more thing I'll have to buy you," she told Magic as she buckled the surcingles around his belly, "a nice blue sweat sheet to match the new blanket." Straightening, she snapped a lead onto his halter. "Come on. I'll walk you a few more minutes."

She led the horse to the new barn. The overhead lights were on, but it was quiet. Stepping inside, she halted him in the concrete aisle.

"Look at this," she said with a sweep of her arm. "This is where you'll be living pretty soon. Isn't it grand?"

Magic reached out his nose toward a stall door. Andie led him closer. It was empty.

"This exact stall might even be yours!" she told him. "I'll get a brass nameplate to put over the door that says Mr. Magic. And under your name it will say Owned by Andie Perez."

Owned by Andie Perez. Just thinking about it made shivers race down Andie's back.

Magic nudged her arm, then pulled her toward the next stall. It was empty, too, but bedded with fresh straw. Sticking his head over the stall door, the Thoroughbred blew loudly.

"This is Superstar's stall. I guess he's out in his paddock." Andie looked down the aisle. "I wonder where Jina is? I hope she's busy cleaning tack."

Turning, Andie led Magic toward the small tack room. The clip-clop of his horseshoes on the concrete echoed through the barn. A bird fluttered in the rafters. Straw rustled.

Grinning happily, Andie took a deep breath. She loved this place.

"Jina?" she called softly, rapping on the tack room door.

"What?" came the muffled reply.

Andie opened the door. When she swung it wide, Magic threw up his head and backed several steps. "Whoa, silly," Andie crooned.

Jina stood beside a cleaning hook which hung from the ceiling. Leather reins were draped over one of the hook's prongs, and a bucket of water was on the floor. Andie could smell glycerin saddle soap and neat's-foot oil.

"Working hard?" Andie greeted her roommate.

Jina didn't answer. Instead, she swung around and threw a sponge in the bucket. Magic snorted again.

"Take it easy, dopey," Andie said. "It's just Jina. She's not that scary."

"Oh, yeah?" Jina growled. "In a second I'm going to start screaming bloody murder."

"What's wrong?"

Jina put her soapy hands on her hips. "Oh, Ashley gave me tack to clean, all right. But it must be stuff she's been storing in a manure pile. It's filthy and the leather's all dry and cracked."

Andie shrugged. "Then I'll just charge her more. Keep track of your time."

Jina blew out her breath. "Don't worry. I might even add an hour." She grinned sneakily.

Suddenly a piercing scream ripped through the stillness of the barn. Andie jumped, startling Magic. He spun sideways, pulling the lead through her fingers.

She caught the strap just as another scream echoed through the barn. Jina ran to the doorway, a rag clutched in her fingers.

"That sounds like Mary Beth!" Jina gasped.

Andie clapped her hand to her mouth. "Oh no!" she exclaimed. "I bet it *is* Mary Beth. She was supposed to be grooming Snowman. Something terrible must have happened!"

9

Clucking to Magic, Andie ran down the aisle to the other side of the barn. Jina raced beside her as they rounded the corner.

When they reached Snowman's stall, Andie stopped and peered in. Magic halted next to her, his shoes clanking and scraping on the concrete.

Snowman, a tall gray horse, stood in front of the door, his tail to Andie. A lead strap dangled from his halter. His ears were pinned back as he stared suspiciously at Mary Beth, who was plastered against the back wall.

"Mary Beth! Are you all right?" Jina asked breathlessly. She was leaning over the door next to Andie, trying to see around the gray horse.

"No!" Mary Beth gasped. Her back was to the wall, her arms stretched wide as if she were holding it up. A brush lay at her feet. "I'm not all right!"

"What happened?" Andie thrust Magic's lead at Jina and unlatched the stall door.

"He—he won't let me out," Mary Beth stammered, still frozen against the wall. Tears welled in her eyes. "When I finished brushing him, I started to unsnap the lead, but he spun around and blocked the door."

"Don't panic." Andie tried to push the door open, but it hit Snowman's hind leg. "Hey, you oaf, get your fat self out of my way."

"Don't!" Mary Beth screeched. "If he turns around, he'll kick me!"

"Kick you?" Puzzled, Andie glanced at Jina. "Is Snowman a kicker?" she asked in a low voice.

Jina frowned. "I don't think so," she whispered back. "Remember when Mary Beth's little sister took a nap in his stall? He didn't hurt her. And Stacey never seems to have a problem."

Andie turned back to Mary Beth. She was about to tell Finney not to be such a wimp.

But one glance at her roommate's trembling lower lip and red-rimmed eyes told her she really was scared.

"Okay. Don't worry, Mary Beth," Andie said, squeezing through the partly open door. Snowman swung his head around, his ears still flattened threateningly.

Andie scowled at him. "Cut it out, you bully," she said, snatching up the dangling strap. As soon as she had it in her hand, his ears perked up.

Mary Beth's shoulders sagged with relief. "Thanks, Andie."

Jina opened the stall door wider. Andie stood by Snowman's head, holding the halter tight. As Mary Beth inched cautiously toward the door, Andie moved the big horse out of the way.

"He's all right now, Mary Beth," she said, scratching his forehead to prove it. "And you did a nice job brushing him. Stacey should be really pleased."

Mary Beth sniffed loudly. "I don't care. I'm never going to brush him again. I never want to brush *any* strange horse again," she declared. "Only Dan. For the rest of my life."

Andie rolled her eyes, and Snowman

rubbed his nose on her shoulder. As far as she could tell, he *was* a pussycat, just as she'd told Mary Beth. She had no idea why he had acted up.

"Okay, I won't give you any more horses to clean. How about tack? That doesn't bite."

Mary Beth frowned. "Laugh all you want, Andie, but I'm telling you, Snowman was out to get me," she retorted. Turning abruptly, she stomped down the aisle.

"Maybe he liked your carrot-colored hair," Andie called.

"Give her a break," Jina said. "Mary Beth's just not used to working around horses much."

Andie sighed. "You're right. Sometimes I forget she's only a beginner." She reached over the stall door. "Hand me Snowman's blanket. We don't want Stacey to think we didn't finish our job."

When the blanket was buckled, Andie took off Snowman's halter. Immediately, he moved to the far corner of his stall.

"He really isn't very friendly," she told Jina as she slipped out the door, latching it behind her, "not like Magic."

Jina gave her Magic's lead. "I hope he didn't scare Mary Beth too badly. I think I'll go check on her." She started down the aisle.

"What about Ashley's tack?"

Jina turned and walked backward a few steps. "I'll finish it later. Mary Beth's more important right now."

"Hey, wait a minute," Andie started to protest, but Jina had already rounded the corner. Andie shook her head in disgust. When would her roommates understand? There wasn't anything more important right now than these jobs.

Because the jobs meant money. And money would buy her Magic.

Andie stroked the Thoroughbred's soft muzzle, then felt under his sweat sheet. He was cool and dry.

It was time to put him away. She had to go see those girls about cleaning their tack. After that she'd head back to the dorm to make a schedule for tomorrow. Then there were the rest of the snacks to bag and—

The list went on and on. Running a business sure was hard work, Andie decided.

"But it's definitely worth it," she assured Magic. "Because it won't be long before you're mine!"

*   *   *

"Okay, guys. Listen up." Andie glanced down at her notebook. Shoulder to shoulder, her three roommates stood at mock attention in front of her.

It was six o'clock Thursday morning. The girls had gotten up extra early so they could finish their morning jobs before classes started.

"Mary Beth, you have beds to make in suites 2B, 3B, 2C, 5C, and 1E. Jina, you need to start two loads of laundry, then fold and deliver the clothes we did last night. Lauren, you've got to clean Stephanie and Christina's suite."

"Aye, aye, Captain." Mary Beth saluted sharply. Then she frowned and cocked her head. "What were those suite numbers again?"

Andie sighed in exasperation. "Write them down this time, Finney." She handed the notebook to her roommate. "I really have to make that schedule. We're getting so many jobs it's hard to keep them straight."

"What you really have to do this morning is finish cleaning *our* suite," Jina warned. Working quickly, she began to pull socks from a laundry basket and match them. "Inspection's early, and Shiroo's been on the warpath."

"That's for sure," Mary Beth said. "Remember, we got that warning last week. If we don't pass inspection today"—she ran a finger under her chin as if cutting her throat—"we're dead."

"Yeah, yeah." Andie waved her away. "I told you I'd take care of it."

"You'd better!" Lauren threw over her shoulder as she hurried out the door, carrying a dust rag and floor mop.

Mary Beth handed Andie back the notebook. She'd written the suite numbers on her palm. "Okay. I'm off to make beds. See you guys."

"'Bye." Jina waved a sock in the air.

Flopping back on her unmade bed, Andie studied the list of clients and jobs. Then she went over to her desk and took out a piece of chart paper that she'd gotten the day before at the student supply store. She picked up her ruler and was dividing the paper into three columns when a flying sock landed on top of her head like a hat.

"Hey!" Andie glared over at Jina.

Her roommate giggled. "The new sock look—very chic," Jina teased as she plucked the sock from Andie's head. Bending, she picked up the laundry basket. "I'm leaving, too. Have fun cleaning the suite."

Andie wiggled her fingers good-bye. As soon as Jina left, she sprang off the bed and peered into the hall, looking right, then left.

Stepping back inside the suite, she shut the door, then scurried over to her dresser drawer and pulled out her fanny pack. It jingled with the sound of money.

Grinning gleefully, Andie dumped the money on the bed. All morning, she'd been waiting for this moment. She was dying to find out how much money they'd made since Tuesday night.

It took almost fifteen minutes to sort the bills and coins and add them up. When Andie was through, she fell back against the headboard, amazed.

She couldn't believe it. They'd made fifty dollars!

"Whoopee!" Andie threw a handful of bills in the air, letting them rain over her face. She was halfway to the hundred-dollar deposit she was planning to offer Mrs. Caufield. And fifty dollars closer to owning Magic!

"What's all the cheering about?" The door opened and Mary Beth came into the suite. Startled, Andie swung around.

Looking just as surprised, Mary Beth glanced around the room. Then she whirled and slammed the door behind her.

"What are you doing?" she hissed.

Andie grinned sheepishly. "I was just counting how much money we've made."

"Counting money!" Mary Beth exclaimed. "But Shiroo's down the hall. She'll be here any second to inspect the suite, and you haven't done a thing!"

"Shiroo! Already?" Andie scrambled to her knees and furiously began stuffing money back into the fanny pack.

Mary Beth flew across the room, and she started tossing clothes and shoes into the wardrobe. "If we don't pass inspection this time, we're in major trouble," she said through clenched teeth. "And it will be all your fault, Perez." Straightening, Mary Beth pointed a paddock boot at Andie. "All your fault!"

10

"Don't panic," Andie tried to reassure Mary Beth, even though she was feeling pretty panicky herself. She'd been so excited about counting the money, she'd forgotten all about Shiroo and inspection.

"We'll get it done." Hurriedly, Andie pulled her blanket to the headboard and flopped the pillow on top. Then she raced into the bathroom.

Toothpaste and soap scum dotted the counter and sink. Andie grabbed a towel, wet a corner, and scrubbed. When she'd gotten most of the dirt up, she wiped off the toilet seat, then threw the towel in the cupboard under the sink and slammed the door shut.

"Bathroom's done!" she announced. Mary Beth was on her hands and knees, cleaning dust from under the beds with a mop.

Andie jumped over her back to Lauren's bed. Luckily, Jina's was already made. She pulled up Lauren's pink comforter, then smoothed Mary Beth's quilt. "There!"

Mary Beth gave one more whoosh. The mop handle whacked the leg of Jina's desk. The bookstand slid, and all of Jina's books toppled to the floor.

Andie clapped her palm to her forehead. "Oh, no!" Dropping to her knees, she tried to scoop the books in a pile.

The door opened, and Ms. Shiroo, Bracken Hall's dorm mother, walked in. She wore a white blouse and trim skirt, low heels, and a no-nonsense expression.

"Are you girls ready?" she asked politely, her arched brow the only hint of surprise at seeing them on the floor.

"Uh…" Mary Beth and Andie glanced at each other.

"We had a little accident." Andie pointed to the books.

Ms. Shiroo nodded. "I'll check the bathroom while you're cleaning it up."

When the dorm mother went into the bathroom, Andie let out her breath. Mary Beth helped her stack the books, then ran down the hall to put the mop away. When she came back, Jina and Lauren were with her.

"I told them what happened," Mary Beth whispered to Andie angrily. "I told them you didn't finish cleaning the room!"

Andie cringed. She could tell from the scowls on her roommates' faces that they were definitely not happy.

"Girls!" Ms. Shiroo called.

"Uh-oh," Andie muttered, gulping hard.

"Come on." Mary Beth gave her a push. "We'd better go see what she wants."

Andie stumbled to the doorway and reluctantly peered in. Jina, Mary Beth, and Lauren crowded right behind her.

Ms. Shiroo was pulling the dirty towel from under the sink. Andie could see blue toothpaste and green soap stains on it.

"What's this?" the dorm mother asked.

"We, uh, we use it to wipe our sink clean," Andie explained.

Ms. Shiroo dropped it on the floor. "No. You use a sponge and cleanser. Then maybe this bathroom won't be quite so disgusting."

Disgusting? Andie didn't think it looked *that* bad.

"I hope the rest of the suite looks better," Ms. Shiroo said, sweeping past the girls. Bending at the waist, she glanced under Andie's bed.

Andie lifted her foot, pretending to aim her toe at Ms. Shiroo's backside. Just a little kick would—

A gasp beside her made Andie freeze in midair. She turned to look at Lauren. Her roommate's blue eyes were wide with horror.

Ms. Shiroo straightened up. "There's at least a week's worth of dust under there."

She pulled Andie's blanket to the foot of the bed. The sheet lay wrinkled underneath it. Crossing the room, she did the same to Lauren's and Mary Beth's beds. "And the beds are not made properly."

Mary Beth shot a sharp look at Andie. Andie shrugged her shoulders, trying to act as if she didn't care.

Ms. Shiroo headed for the wardrobe, and all four girls held their breaths. When she opened the door, a riding helmet fell from the top shelf, missing her head by inches.

The dorm mother didn't even blink. "This room obviously does not pass inspection. You girls were warned last week. I will be inspecting your suite again tomorrow morning. If it is not spick-and-span, you will all be brought up before the dorm committee."

"Yes, Ms. Shiroo," Mary Beth, Jina, and Lauren chorused.

Andie squeezed her lips tight, afraid to open her mouth. If she did, she might tell Shiroo to go jump in the Foxhall swimming pool.

When the dorm mother left, Mary Beth threw her arms up in the air. "Oh, great. The *dorm committee*," she wailed. "Those guys will give us Breakfast Club for a week."

"Or worse." Lauren fell backward on her bed. "I've heard the committee made one suite scrub their entire floor with toothbrushes."

"Toothbrushes!" Jina moaned. "My hands are already cracked from cleaning all that tack."

Mary Beth glowered at Andie. "And it's all your fault, Perez."

For a second, Andie wanted to tell her roommates to go jump in the swimming pool, too. Then she slumped down in her desk chair. She knew they were right.

"Okay. I admit it. It was my fault. Tonight and tomorrow I'll clean the whole suite. It'll be spotless, I promise."

For a few moments, no one said a thing. Andie wondered if her roommates would ever speak to her again.

Then Lauren started to giggle. "Were you really going to kick Shiroo, Andie?"

"Well, maybe just a teeny tap," Andie said sheepishly. And when her roommates broke up laughing, she knew things would be okay.

"This is Friday's schedule?" Jina said that evening. The four roommates were standing in the hall outside suite 4B. Earlier, Andie had rushed from the barn to make up the schedule so she could hang it on the door before dinner.

"That's it." Andie grinned proudly.

She glanced at her roommates. Their mouths were hanging open as they stared at the chart taped on the memo board.

"Pretty impressive, huh?" Her smile widened.

Lauren, Jina, and Mary Beth swung their gazes toward Andie. She shifted uncomfortably under their icy glares, and her smile died. Okay, so maybe they weren't so impressed. Maybe they were still mad about this morning's inspection.

"There's no way we can do all that," Mary

Beth protested finally. She pointed to her column. "It was hard enough making six beds this
morning. Tomorrow I'll have to get up at five
A.M. if you expect me to make six beds, plus
clean a bathroom before breakfast."

"Well—" Andie started to explain.

"And when am I supposed to vacuum two
suites *and* pull a mane?" Jina chimed in. "Since
I went to Middlefield this afternoon, I didn't
have time to finish Ashley's tack, so I'll have to
do it tomorrow afternoon."

"Maybe we could—" Andie tried again.

"And I have to meet my tutor at three
tomorrow afternoon, so there's no way I can
groom an extra horse," Lauren cut her off.

Andie threw up her hands. "I know. I know.
It does seem like a lot. But I think we can do
it."

"*We* can do it?" Mary Beth sputtered. "That
brings up an interesting point." Hands on her
hips, she took a step toward Andie. "I see a
column of jobs for me, Lauren, and Jina. Why
isn't *your* name on the list?"

"I can explain that," Andie said quickly. She
held up one finger. "First, I have to clean our
room to get ready for tomorrow's inspection.
And I really will do it this time, I promise. Sec-

ond, I have to check out our clients' suites to make sure you guys did a good job. Third—"

Lauren's jaw dropped. "You don't trust us to do a good job?"

"Of course I do. But the clients expect everything to be perfect. Now, where was I?" Andie stuck up a third finger. "Three, I have to line up more jobs for this weekend. Saturday should be a big day for us, you know. Four, I have to make tomorrow's schedule, and five, I need to print more flyers for Mill Hall. See? I've got lots of important things to do." She wiggled the five fingers in the other girls' faces.

"Oh, really?" Mary Beth pushed Andie's hand away. "It seems to me like you've been doing only *two* big things: getting us in trouble with Shiroo and bossing us around."

"Right," Jina and Lauren chorused.

"When we decided to do this, we didn't think you were going to run us ragged," Jina said. "I mean, we've all got tests and papers and stuff to finish before Thanksgiving."

"And we haven't worked on our English project since Monday," Lauren added. "It's due next week, and Tiffany keeps bugging me about it."

"I'll take care of Tiffany," Andie said. "But,

meanwhile, we've got a busy night. We have the rest of the snacks to bag, and Lauren, after dinner, right before study hours, you need to dust and—"

"Weren't you listening, Andie?" Mary Beth cut in impatiently. "We can't do all your stupid jobs."

Stupid jobs! Andie stared in disbelief at her roommates. Arms crossed, Jina was scowling down at her feet. Mary Beth's mouth was set in a stubborn line, and Lauren was frowning and biting her lip at the same time.

As Andie took in their determined expressions, a dull ache grew in her stomach. Her roommates had stuck by her through a lot of crazy stuff. But now, when she needed them the most, they were going to let her down.

They weren't going to help her buy Magic!

11

"Sorry, Andie," Jina said finally, still looking down at her feet. "We want to help you, but we've got our own homework to finish and horses to take care of. There just isn't enough time to do it all."

Lauren and Mary Beth nodded in agreement. A group of girls wearing Foxhall blazers came down the hall, passing behind Andie on their way to dinner. They glanced curiously at the four roommates but kept walking.

Panic clutched Andie's insides. Her mind raced. She *had* to think of a way to convince her roommates to keep helping her.

"Guys, listen to me," Andie pleaded. "You can't quit now. When I came back to the suite this afternoon, I counted up the money in my fanny pack. So far, we've made seventy-five dollars, not counting the ten Ashley still owes us. So we've made eighty-five dollars and we haven't even sold tonight's snacks yet!"

Lauren raised one brow. "We've made eighty-five dollars since Tuesday?"

Andie nodded excitedly. "Isn't that super? So you've got to hang in there a little longer. *Please.*"

"You're crazy, Andie." Jina shook her head. "Eighty-five dollars isn't even close to a thousand. And that's how much you need to buy Magic."

Andie clutched Jina's wrist. "But all I need right now is a hundred. Just fifteen more dollars. Then I can give Mrs. Caufield a deposit on Magic so Melanie Harden can't get her witch's claws in him."

Andie's gaze zigzagged from roommate to roommate.

"Well…" Mary Beth hesitated. Tilting her head, she looked at Jina. Jina looked at Lauren. Then Lauren looked back at Mary Beth, who finally nodded. "Okay," she said.

Andie grabbed her in a bear hug and squeezed her hard. Then, whooping and cheering, she hugged Jina and Lauren.

"But no more bossing us around," Mary

Beth warned, frowning at Andie.

"Promise. Scout's honor." Andie slapped her hand over her heart. "I pledge on the flag and all that."

"And you've got to make sure our suite passes inspection," Lauren said sternly. "There's no way I want to go before that dorm committee."

Andie bobbed her head. "No problem."

Jina tapped the memo board. "And you're going to have to take some of these chores off today's chart. We're not superwomen, you know."

"Right." Andie grinned playfully. "You're better than superwomen. You're super roomies!"

Friday afternoon, Andie raced up the hill to the barn. She was late for her lesson. But for once she didn't care.

She'd just finished printing out the flyers for Mill Hall. Even more important, she'd counted the money the girls had made since they'd started their business. Now she was dying to tell Jina, Lauren, and Mary Beth the good news. They'd made a hundred dollars!

Halfway up the hill, Andie slowed to catch

her breath. It was another crisp, sunny day. The two outdoor rings were filled with horses and riders. She glimpsed Mary Beth practicing a sitting trot on Dan in the first ring. In the second ring, Lauren cantered Whisper.

Disappointed, Andie stuck out her lower lip. She'd have to wait to tell them after their lessons. Then her face brightened with excitement. She could still tell Magic the good news—that soon he'd be hers!

Okay, so it will probably take forever to earn nine hundred dollars more, Andie thought as she sprinted up the hill. But at least she had a deposit now. Tomorrow, she'd take the money to Mrs. Caufield. It would prove that she was serious about buying Magic.

Andie flew across the grassy courtyard. It was surprisingly empty. She hadn't realized she was that late for her lesson.

"Magic!" Andie called. Reaching his stall, she dropped her helmet on a bale of straw, then threw back the latch. "Magic, guess—" Her voice died as she swung open the bottom door.

Magic was gone!

Frantically, Andie glanced around the courtyard. Where could he be?

The pasture! Andie exhaled with relief. Usually Dorothy brought all the horses in before lessons. Today she must have forgotten.

Grabbing a lead, Andie ran around to the back of the barn. She stopped, stared across the pasture, and whistled. But the pasture was empty, too.

"Andie!" someone called.

Andie whirled around. Jina was hurrying toward her, leading Superstar. She'd taken off the gray horse's blanket, and his dappled coat was shining in the winter sun. In September, Superstar had sprained a tendon. His leg was healing, but Jina still had to walk him every day.

"I have a message for you." Jina puffed as she drew closer. "Mrs. Caufield said to tell you that Magic's already tacked up and in the indoor ring."

"He is? Why?"

Jina shrugged. Superstar pulled his head down, trying to reach a clump of brown grass. "I don't know. Maybe Lauren told them you were going to be late."

"Yeah. That must be it." Andie patted the gray's silky neck. "But I've been riding with Mary Beth's group, and today they're in the outdoor ring. I wonder why Magic's in the indoor ring?" Puzzled, she thought for a second, then grinned. "Hey, I bet Caufield's going to have Magic and me do something special this afternoon."

"Maybe." Jina smiled wistfully. Andie knew that Jina missed riding Superstar. At least her roommate had Applejacks, the Chamberses' pony. But since he was boarded at Middlefield Stables, it wasn't the same.

"I have good news," Andie told Jina as they started back around the barn. "We made a hundred dollars!"

Jina stopped in her tracks. "You're kidding! We really did?"

Andie nodded excitedly. "So now I can put that deposit on Magic. I can't wait to tell Lauren and Mary Beth. Maybe I can convince them to keep working now. What do you think?"

"I don't know." Jina shrugged. "We've all got so much to do before Thanksgiving break."

"Oh. Right. I understand." Andie tried not to sound too disappointed. She didn't dare tell Jina about the flyers she'd printed for Mill Hall. Maybe she'd have to forget about passing them out.

"Well, thanks for the message. I'll see you after lessons." With a wave, Andie jogged down the covered aisle to Magic's stall. She picked up her riding helmet, then headed toward the indoor ring.

Her disappointment faded as she neared the ring. After all, she couldn't really blame her roommates. Cleaning rooms and making beds was no fun. And they had worked hard when it really counted.

Besides, she was getting too excited about this afternoon to be upset. It was time she quit riding with the baby beginners. Maybe during this afternoon's lesson, Mrs. Caufield would let her trot Magic over a small jump. That would be so cool!

Andie had longed Magic over poles, so she knew he could jump. She'd also trotted him over a small crossbar to show her dad what a super horse he was. Unfortunately, she'd fallen off, badly bruisng her knee. It had hurt like crazy, but she'd never forget how high he'd jumped—like Pegasus soaring into the sky.

When Andie reached the indoor ring, butterflies fluttered in her stomach. The huge area was swarming with girls and horses. At first, she couldn't see Mrs. Caufield. Then she spotted the director in the far corner. But she wasn't holding a horse.

Standing on tiptoes, Andie peered anxiously around the ring. Where was Magic?

Then she saw him. He was trotting in a small circle around Mrs. Caufield, and *there was another girl riding him!*

Anger swelled and stuck in Andie's throat. How could Caufield let someone else on her horse? Then she inhaled sharply, almost choking when she realized who the rider was— Melanie Harden!

12

"Get off my horse, Melanie," Andie muttered. Furious, she stormed across the indoor ring, dodging startled horses and riders.

"Watch out!" someone hollered as a horse thundered past, narrowly missing Andie.

"Watch out yourself," Andie growled without slowing. Her eyes were locked on Melanie Harden, following her every move as she trotted Magic around Mrs. Caufield.

"Andie!" Mrs. Caufield called sternly. "Don't cross the ring in the middle of lessons. Wait by the exit gate. I'll bring Magic over when Melanie's finished."

Andie shook her head in an angry no. Stomping around two horses, she halted in front of the riding director.

"Why is Melanie riding my horse?" she

demanded angrily.

"Excuse me?" Mrs. Caufield raised her brows and looked down at Andie. "Were you speaking to *me* in that rude tone of voice?" She pointed to herself with feigned surprise.

Andie flushed bright red. Mrs. Caufield's curt reply was like a slap in the face. But she knew she deserved it. She was out of line talking to the riding director that way.

"I'm sorry," Andie apologized quickly. "It's just that I'm really upset that Melanie's riding my horse."

Turning, Andie watched as the older girl slowed Magic to a walk. A triumphant smile played across Melanie's lips when she saw Andie looking at her.

Mrs. Caufield patted Andie's arm. "I know you're upset. But Melanie's been nagging me to try him. And, remember, Magic isn't your horse. So when Lauren told me you were going to be late, I thought this might be a good time."

"But he's mine to ride this semester," Andie protested.

"True," Mrs. Caufield said, nodding. "But even though you're leasing him, he still belongs to Foxhall."

"Only you can't sell him to Melanie," Andie

91

declared. "*I'm* going to buy him! Soon!"

Mrs. Caufield squeezed her shoulder. "Calm down, Andie. If you'd quit being such a hot-head and actually watch Melanie ride Magic, I think you'll feel better."

Andie bit her lip, forcing back her anger. Reluctantly, she turned to face Melanie and Magic again.

The senior had reversed direction. She was a good rider, but Andie immediately noticed a lot of things she was doing wrong with Magic. Her hands were heavy on the reins, and the more the Thoroughbred fidgeted, the tighter she held them. And though she sat straight and tall in the saddle, Melanie's back was rigid and her legs were clamped hard against his sides like a vise.

"Melanie," Mrs. Caufield called, "I told you to use light hands and legs on this horse. If you don't, he's going to act up."

Melanie nodded, but Andie could tell she wasn't listening. When she signaled Magic to trot, her body stiffened and her fingers closed around the reins.

Magic broke into an uneven trot. His lower lip flapped, and he shook his head with unbridled nervous energy.

Relax your body, loosen your reins, make a small circle, Andie wanted to tell Melanie. *Then pat him and tell him it's okay.*

But Melanie only rode him more forcefully. Using her seat and legs, she drove him forward. Magic's ears flipped back and forth in confusion. "He's not listening," Melanie said through gritted teeth.

"That's because you're not telling him the right way. Use light aids and voice," Mrs. Caufield replied.

Instead, Melanie shortened the reins. Magic tucked his chin into his neck, trying to avoid the harsh tug on the bit. Then he began to bounce up and down like a broken hobbyhorse.

Melanie's cheeks reddened with anger. Pulling sharply with one rein, she turned him in a semicircle.

Andie couldn't stand it any longer. "Stop that!" she yelled, running toward them.

Magic halted. His neck was bent awkwardly toward Melanie's right stirrup. Andie could see the fear in his eyes.

Darting forward, she grabbed the left rein from Melanie. *You jerk!* she wanted to shout, but before she could say anything to the snobby girl, Mrs. Caufield came up.

"I think that's enough, Melanie," she said calmly. "Magic's obviously too green for what you want to do."

"That's for sure." Dropping the rein, Melanie glared at Andie before dismounting. Andie glared right back. Magic shook his head, his mane flying.

"I'm looking for a horse I can start eventing this spring," Melanie told Mrs. Caufield, ignoring Andie's nasty looks. "This horse doesn't know the basic aids and he can't even move forward at a decent trot. He definitely won't work for me."

Andie's shoulders sagged with relief. She was never so glad to hear bad things about a horse in her life.

Shaking her head, Melanie walked off with Mrs. Caufield. Andie gave Magic a weary hug. "Are you all right?" she asked, stroking his sweaty neck. He pushed her with his nose, almost knocking her over, then started to pull her toward the exit.

"Hey! Lessons aren't over." Andie grinned as she looped the reins around her arm so she could put on her helmet. "We've still got work to do, buddy. Luckily, Melanie has zoomed off on her witch's broom, so she won't be riding you—ever again." Andie gave him a reassuring pat. "I promise."

"Are you ready to walk back to the suite?" Mary Beth asked later that afternoon, poking her head over Magic's stall door. "Lauren and Jina left already."

"Not quite," Andie replied. She was bent over, checking the front strap on the blanket. It was beginning to tear away from the quilted fabric. "I have to talk to Caufield first."

Mary Beth's face lit up. "Are you going to give her the deposit?"

Andie nodded. "The sooner the better. It scared me to death when I saw Melanie riding Magic." She grinned. "Scared *him* to death, too. He'd never been ridden by a witch before."

"She can't be that bad."

"Oh, yes she can. Just ask Magic." Andie scratched the star on the Throughbred's forehead, and several white hairs fell on the sleeve of her jacket. Reaching down, she picked up his grooming kit.

"So what do you think Caufield will say?" Stepping aside, Mary Beth opened the stall door so Andie could come out.

Andie frowned. "She'll say yes, of course. She knows Magic should be my horse."

"I can't believe it will be that easy," Mary Beth said doubtfully. "I mean, it's not like your dad's buying him. You're just a kid. Why would she sell him to you?"

Andie swung the door shut with a sharp bang. "I don't know," she snapped, "but she will."

Puffing angrily, she turned sharply and crossed the courtyard. The sky was dark, and most of the girls had already left. Out of the corner of her eye, she saw Mary Beth start down the hill toward the campus. Her hands were shoved in her jacket pockets, and her neck was hunched into her collar.

Sorry I yelled at you, Mary Beth, Andie told her roommate silently. The truth was she had a feeling that Mary Beth was right. Caufield probably wouldn't accept a hundred-dollar deposit from a kid, no matter how much she wanted to buy the horse.

When Andie reached the office door, she knocked hesitantly.

"Come in!" Mrs. Caufield said.

Slowly, Andie opened the door and peered inside. Her mind flashed back to the first time she'd entered the riding director's office to talk about Magic. She'd been just as scared then. But the first time she'd been scared because she'd broken a rule.

This time she was scared that, after all her and her roommates' hard work, she might not get to own Magic after all.

Mrs. Caufield was sitting at her desk chair, the phone receiver stuck between her cheek and shoulder. Her coat, hat, and boots were draped over the desk.

"Yes, I understand," the director was saying into the receiver. She gestured for Andie to sit down on a chair in front of her desk.

Andie undid the top button on her coat and pulled off her ear warmers. Then she perched nervously at the edge of the chair.

"Yes, Andie?" Mrs. Caufield said as she finished her call and hung up the phone.

Andie sat up straighter in the chair. "I wanted to ask about buying Magic."

"Okay. Ask."

"I'd like to put a deposit on him. A hundred dollars. I thought that might hold him until the semester was up and we could pay you the rest."

Mrs. Caufield looked pleased. "How nice.

97

Your dad finally came around and decided to buy Magic? What a nice surprise."

Andie didn't answer. Ducking her head, she reached under her jacket and unbuckled the fanny pack. She'd been wearing it all day. "I have the money right here," she said, unzipping the pack. Mrs. Caufield raised her eyebrows, but she didn't say anything.

Finally, when Andie started counting out dollar bills, the director held up her hand. "Whoa there! You have a hundred dollars in *ones?*"

"No," Andie replied. "I've got a few fives and a ten."

Leaning forward, Mrs. Caufield frowned. "I'm not sure I understand, Andie. I thought your dad was putting a deposit on Magic."

Andie hesitated, her heart racing.

She scanned the riding director's face, looking for a sign that she would let her buy Magic. But deep down, Andie knew there wouldn't be any sign. She'd been stupid to think a grown-up would ever, ever understand.

Taking a deep breath, Andie looked Mrs. Caufield directly in the eyes. "That's right. My father is buying Magic," she fibbed smoothly. Then, without blinking, she held out the money.

13

Mrs. Caufield didn't move.

Take it, Andie urged silently, tears welling in her eyes. *Take the money!* Finally, she sighed and her hand fell limply to her lap.

"Okay. My dad hasn't agreed to buy Magic," she said, swiping at her damp cheeks. "But he will. He'll see what a super horse he is."

Mrs. Caufield smiled gently. "And he'll see how determined his daughter is, too. Listen, Andie, hang on to your money. Maybe there is some way you can put a deposit on Magic."

Andie's chin snapped up. "Really?"

Mrs. Caufield shrugged, but her smile broadened. "Why not? Foxhall Academy prides itself on innovative programs designed to help each girl reach her potential. We just may be able to work something out. Of course," she added sternly, "this would have to be with your father's approval."

"Of course!" Andie agreed, grinning back at Mrs. Caufield.

"I've never seen someone quite so intent on buying a horse," the riding director admitted. "And you've certainly proved to me that you're responsible enough to own your own horse."

Responsible enough to own your own horse. Andie almost choked. She'd been waiting to hear those words her whole life.

"Thank you!" she said gratefully.

"Okay," Mrs. Caufield said. "Get back to your suite so you don't miss dinner. I'll talk to Dean Wilkes. Maybe we can all meet tomorrow."

Andie sprang from her chair. "That sounds great! And thank you, *thank you!*"

Ten minutes later, Andie raced up the stairs to the fourth floor of Bracken Hall. She was so excited that she was sure she'd burst if she didn't tell someone.

Lauren was in the hall, talking on the phone. Andie ran up behind her.

"He's mine. He's mine!" she sang in her roommate's ear.

"Who?" Lauren asked, looking puzzled.

"Magic!"

Lauren squealed and gave Andie the thumbs-up sign. Quickly, she covered the receiver with her palm. "That's super, Andie. Tell the others. They're in the room, waiting to go to dinner. Oh, and tell Mary Beth that I'm talking to Tommy."

"Right." Twirling and humming, Andie tap-danced all the way up the hall, her boot soles clumping against the tile.

Mary Beth, Jina, and Tiffany Dubray were sitting in a circle on Jina's bed, wearing their Foxhall blazers.

"Ta-da!" Andie threw her arms wide. "You are now looking at the new almost-owner of a horse!"

"Great!" Jina grinned excitedly. "So all that hard work was worth it, huh?"

"Congratulations, roomie." Mary Beth jumped off the bed and whacked Andie hard on the back. "What did you do, tie Caufield up and torture her until she said yes?"

Tiffany cocked her head. "You're really buying a horse, Andie?" she asked, tugging on a lock of blond hair.

Andie nodded and fell back on her bed. "I'm buying the most wonderful horse in the whole wide world," she said with a happy sigh.

Then a shadow fell over her. Andie peered up to see Mary Beth standing over her, arms crossed.

"So did Mrs. Caufield actually take the money?" she asked.

"Well, no," Andie admitted. "I'm meeting with her tomorrow."

"Hmm." Mary Beth said between her lips.

Andie squinted up at her. "What does 'hmm' mean?"

"Well, it sounds to me like you don't exactly own Magic yet."

Andie bolted upright. "It sounds to *me* like you don't know what you're talking about, Finney. Why don't you get lost? Go talk to wimpy Tommy. He's on the phone."

"Tommy?" Mary Beth asked, arms dropping to her sides. "He's on the phone?"

"Gee, is there an echo in here? Yes, he's on the phone." Andie waved toward the hall. "Lauren's talking to him."

"Lauren?" Mary Beth screwed up her face. "Why is *she* talking to him?"

Andie shrugged. "I don't know. Go and ask her yourself!"

"I will!" Mary Beth shouted. Turning, she stomped from the suite, slamming the door behind her.

Andie made a noise of disgust. Then she noticed that Jina and Tiffany weren't saying anything. The two of them were looking at her questioningly.

"Okay, so Magic isn't exactly mine yet," she told them. "But he will be. Caufield almost promised. And she's pretty decent for a grown-up."

"We believe you," Jina said, "but what about your dad?"

Andie scowled. "What about him?"

"Won't he have to give his permission?"

"Well, yeah. But he will. He'll be so impressed when I tell him how much money we earned, he'll just have to say it's okay. I mean, that's what he admires most—ruthless businesspeople."

Jina chuckled. "And you are definitely ruthless."

"So *that's* why you were doing all that work,

selling snacks and making beds," Tiffany said, tapping her chin.

Andie nodded. "And we've made a hundred dollars. So far."

"A hundred dollars." Tiffany furrowed her brow. "Is that how much a horse costs?"

Andie rolled her eyes. "Boy, Tiff, you're even dumber about horses than Finney."

Just then the door swung open and Lauren marched into the room. Her expression was stormy.

"Hungry?" Andie teased.

"No. Just mad." Lauren dropped down on the desk chair. "Mary Beth jerked the phone out of my hand while I was talking to Tommy. She was all bent out of shape about it."

"Boo hoo, another fight over wimpy Tommy." Andie drooped her lips in a pretend pout. "No wonder you're depressed."

"Oh, shut up." Lauren grabbed a notebook and threw it at Andie. Andie threw it right back.

Lauren ducked and the notebook hit Tiffany on the nose.

"Ow!" Tiffany protested. "That hurt." She leaned down and picked up the notebook. "Hey, this is mine. I wrote our play in it. You know, the play about Black Beauty that *I'm* doing all the work on?"

"Oh, quit whining, Tiffany," Andie said. "We'll help you finish it after dinner."

Jina stood up. "Are you guys ready to go?"

"Almost." Andie went over to the wardrobe and began to hunt for her blazer. "Actually, I'm starved. All this wheeling and dealing stuff has made me hungry."

"Well, don't eat any dessert tonight," Jina said.

"Why not?" Andie and Lauren asked together.

Jina shrugged. "I think we should have a party. You know, to celebrate Andie's almost owning a horse."

Andie's face brightened. "Yeah!"

"That's a good idea," Lauren agreed. "I mean, how long has it been since we had a party?"

Andie thought for a moment. "A day or two," she joked.

"But what about the English project?" Tiffany reminded them in a whiny voice. "We were going to do that after dinner. It's due next week, remember?"

"English project?" Andie frowned in pretend confusion. "Do we have an English pro-ject?"

"Yeah, but I'd rather have a party," Lauren said.

"Me too," Jina agreed. "And I have just the right snacks." Reaching under Mary Beth's bed, she pulled out a tan paper-covered shoe-box. An address label was taped on the front. "This package came for Mary Beth today."

"Finney's mom sent more cookies already?" Lauren exclaimed.

Andie's mouth started to water. Even Tiffany eyed the package hungrily.

Lauren glanced hesitantly at Andie. "But don't you want to sell those cookies? I mean, I know we got the deposit, but how are you going to come up with the rest of the money for Magic?"

"Well..." Andie hesitated. "I don't really know. But my ruthless business mind will come up with some brilliant plan."

"Hey, what are you guys doing with my package?" Mary Beth stood in the doorway, hands on her hips.

"We're having a party after dinner to cele-brate Andie's almost owning Magic," Jina explained. "And we're going to eat all your mom's cookies."

"And *then* we're working on the English project," Tiffany declared firmly. Jina, Lauren, and Andie started laughing. Even Mary Beth joined in.

Still laughing, Andie plopped back on the bed to pull off her riding boots. But a nagging fear made her smile fade.

What if her dad wouldn't give her permission to buy Magic?

Andie frowned and tossed her boot on the floor. He *had* to say it was okay. She'd tell him about the flyers she'd made, the schedule she'd set up, and how hard she and her roommates had worked. Then she'd outline a plan for earning the rest of the money.

He'd be so proud of her. And when she told him that Mrs. Caufield thought she was responsible enough to own a horse, he'd smile and give her a big hug and tell her that of course she could buy Magic.

Andie sighed. In her heart, she knew that was just a dream. A dream she desperately wanted to come true.

14

"Why are Saturdays so wonderful?" Lauren asked from her bed.

Andie grunted and opened one eye. The morning sun was streaming through the curtained window, making a shadowy pattern across her blanket.

"I know why *this* Saturday is so wonderful," Jina said. "It's nine o'clock and we're still in bed."

"That's true," Mary Beth agreed. She was lying on her side, her head propped on her hand. "This is the first Saturday we've been able to sleep as long as we want. Remember last Saturday?"

"How could we forget!" Lauren groaned. "I was up at five A.M. getting ready for the horse show."

"And the Saturday before that we had Parents' Weekend and Finneys were everywhere," Andie added. She rolled onto her back and stared up at the ceiling.

That had been the weekend she'd first ridden Magic for her father. She'd been so excited to show the Thoroughbred off. Only everything had gone wrong. Magic had dumped her and she'd bruised her knee. That's when her dad had decided that he would *never* buy Magic.

But it had also been the weekend her father told her he loved her.

Abruptly, Andie sat up. Hope soared in her chest. *Did he love her enough to change his mind about Magic?* Throwing back the blanket, Andie jumped out of bed. "I've got to call my dad," she told the others as she stuck her feet in her moccasins.

"What for?" Jina peeked over her comforter, her golden eyes still sleepy.

"I've got to convince him to let me buy Magic before I meet with Caufield."

Mary Beth groaned and fell back on her pillow. "You never give up, do you, Andie?"

"Never." Andie swung open the suite door. The hall was busy with girls dressed in sweatpants and jeans. Since it was the weekend before Thanksgiving break, hardly any of the students had gone home.

Andie headed for the hall phone. Quickly, she dialed her dad's number. He picked it up on the first ring.

"Dad? It's Andie." She hesitated a second, remembering Sunday night's phone call. She'd been so furious, she'd hung up on him. "How are you?"

"Great," her father replied in his hoarse morning voice. "In fact, I was just going to call you. I've got to go into the office for a while, so how about if I pick you up afterward? We can have a late lunch together."

"Yes!" Andie blurted out excitedly. "I mean, sure, that's a good idea. Listen, I'm sorry for hanging up on you Sunday. But you really made me mad."

"I know." Her father cleared his throat. "And I'm sorry, too."

" So what time will you pick me up? I'll have to get permission."

"About one."

"Okay. And, uh, Dad..." Andie tugged nervously on the phone cord. "When we come back from eating, I'd like you to do something

110

for me. I want you to watch me ride Magic, then talk to Mrs. Caufield."

There was a long silence. Andie held her breath. She could hear the *whoosh-whoosh* of her father's breathing.

"Say yes?" she pleaded.

"All right." He sighed loudly. "I don't want you accusing me of being a stubborn old man."

Andie grinned. "Stubborn? Gee, I'd never call my terrific dad something like that!"

Still grinning, she said good-bye and hung up. Then, twirling in a circle, she floated giddily down the hall and into the suite. Everything was going to work out!

Jina was still in bed, reading a book. Mary Beth stood in front of an open dresser drawer, a turtleneck in her hand. Lauren sat cross-legged on her bed, braiding her hair.

All three looked expectantly at Andie when she came into the suite.

"From her zombie state, I'd say she's either sleepwalking or her father said yes," Lauren said.

Mary Beth snorted. "Maybe all those cookies she ate last night went to her brain."

Andie just grinned and flopped on Jina's bed.

"Ouch. Those are my legs under there." Jina pulled her feet up, then asked, "So what did he say?"

"We're having lunch together. And after that, he's agreed to talk to Caufield."

Jina gasped. "You're kidding! That's terrific."

"I'll say." Lauren secured the end of her braid with a band.

"And this time, nothing's going to go wrong," Andie added. She was feeling more determined than ever. "First, I'm going to show my father how wonderful Magic is. Next, I'm going to tell him about our business and all the money we earned so I can buy Magic. Then, to top off the whole thing, I'm going to have Caufield tell him how responsible she thinks I am. How does that plan sound?"

"Good," Mary Beth said, pulling out sweatpants to go with her turtleneck. Lauren nodded in agreement.

"I think it's better than good," Jina said.

Andie looked at her in surprise. Jina usually wasn't very enthusiastic about her plans. "You do?"

"Yep." Jina shut her book. "You've got it all thought out. I don't know how your father can say no."

"Oh, he can find a way to say no." Andie sighed deeply. "But let's hope you're right."

"Boy, do you look handsome, Mr. Magic!" Andie called from her perch on the top rail of the pasture fence. Jina sat beside her. Mary Beth and Lauren stood on her other side, looking over the fence.

In the middle of the pasture, Magic snorted and pawed at the frozen ground. Andie had taken off his blanket, and in the sun his mahogany-colored coat glistened with browns and reds. Beside him, his buddy, Three Bars Jake, grazed contentedly on the dry winter grass.

A stiff breeze blew around the corner of the barn, and the bare tree limbs whipped back and forth. Throwing up his head, Magic took off in a high-stepping trot. His neck was arched and his tail streamed behind him.

He twisted and bucked. Then with a loud snort, he charged across the pasture, skidding to a halt right in front of Jake. The quarter horse didn't even lift his head.

Andie and her roommates laughed at Magic's antics.

"He does look super," Jina said.

"Let's just hope my dad thinks so," Andie said. "When he gets here, I want him to see Magic running around the pasture. Not that my dad appreciates a horse that's a good mover."

"*Anybody* could see that he's a gorgeous mover," Lauren said.

"Even me," Mary Beth chimed in. "And I don't even know what that means."

Andie jumped off the fence. "I hope he gets here soon." Anxiously she cracked a knuckle, then shoved her cold hands in her pockets.

"It's almost one o'clock," Lauren said, checking her watch. "We'd better get to the cafeteria before they close up. Will you be all right waiting for your dad alone?" she asked Andie.

"Sure," Andie replied. "I'll walk down with you. I'm meeting him at the administration building. I need to sign out."

The four girls hurried down the hill toward the main buildings. When they reached Old House, Andie turned to say good-bye to her roommates.

"Good luck," Jina said, squeezing her arm.

Just then the double doors opened and an older woman, a cardigan sweater draped around her shoulders like a cape, stepped out. It was Mrs. Krabbitz, the secretary for the dean of students.

"You're just the girls I need to see." Mrs. Krabbitz glared at them over her half glasses. "Mrs. Caufield and Dean Wilkes would like to meet with the four of you."

"All of us?" Mary Beth asked in surprise.

Mrs. Krabbitz nodded curtly, then opened the door wider. "Hurry, please. I don't want to stand here all day."

Andie led the way into the administration building. Old House had been built in 1889, when Foxhall Academy was established. Then it had housed classrooms. Now, over a hundred years later, the faculty used it for offices.

"What do you think Wilkes wants with all of us?" Lauren whispered as the girls walked down the wide sunlit hall. The hardwood floors gleamed, and the heavy oak doors and crown molding gave the whole place an old-fashioned look.

Andie shrugged. "Caufield must have told her how we earned all that money. Maybe she wants to congratulate us on our hard work."

"That must be it." Mary Beth nodded enthusiastically. "We're entrepreneurs."

"Come on, girls." Mrs. Krabbitz clapped her hands and herded them into the dean's outer office. "Hurry." She pointed to a partly open door. "Go right on in. They're waiting for you."

Mary Beth glanced over her shoulder at Andie before stepping first into the office. Lauren and Jina were right behind her. Crossing her fingers, Andie walked into the office last.

Dean Wilkes sat behind her desk, looking polished and professional in her tailored suit. Mrs. Caufield stood beside her, wearing jeans and barn boots. Her head was turned and she was staring out the window.

Andie hesitated, then stepped beside Lauren.

"Hello, Andie," a deep voice said.

Andie's gaze darted to the left. *Her father!*

He sat in a chair against the wall, his back rigid, his palms resting on his knees. He was dressed casually in khakis and a navy blue sweater. Andie's mind raced. Why was he in the dean's office? Was it good news? Had they talked already? Had her father decided to buy Magic?

But then she saw that his brow was furrowed and he wasn't smiling. Andie tried to catch his attention. *What's going on?* she wanted to ask him. But his dark eyes wouldn't meet hers. Anxiously, she glanced over at Mrs. Caufield. The riding director continued to stare out the window.

Andie gulped hard, and her palms began to sweat. Suddenly, she knew that Dean Wilkes wasn't going to tell them good news. Her heart plummeted to her toes. She wanted to turn and run from the office.

She'd run away and never come back.

15

"I'm sure you're wondering why I called you all in here," the dean began. Her gaze went from Lauren to Mary Beth to Jina, finally resting on Andie.

Andie couldn't meet her eyes. Her brain felt numb, and she dreaded hearing whatever it was that the dean had to say.

"Yesterday, I found out that you girls have been running a business out of the dorm." Dean Wilkes picked up a piece of paper from the desk. It was one of the flyers Andie had printed, advertising their jobs and rates.

"I realize how hard you girls worked this week and I congratulate you on your entrepreneurial skills. But—" The dean paused.

Andie sucked in her breath. Her fingers were clenched so tightly that her nails dug into her palms. Beside her, Lauren shifted nervously from foot to foot, and Mary Beth cleared her throat. Jina stared straight ahead.

"I'm afraid it is very much against Foxhall rules for any student to receive money from another student unless it's been approved by me." Pushing back the chair, Dean Wilkes stood up. She looked directly at each of the girls, her expression kind. "I'm sorry. I'm afraid your little business is going to have to end."

Andie let out her breath. "We can't even sell snacks?"

Dean Wilkes shook her head. "No. And even more important, I'm afraid you're going to have to give all the money you made back to the girls."

Give the money back! The words pierced Andie's brain like a knife. "But—but—we earned that money so I could buy Magic!" She darted forward and leaned on Dean Wilkes's desk. She had to make the dean understand! "We earned enough to put a deposit on Magic right now," Andie explained frantically. "You can't make me give it back. I'll lose Magic!"

"I'm sorry." Dean Wilkes nodded sympathetically. "Mrs. Caufield told me about the horse. But you'll have to give the money back.

Perhaps you can earn it another way. Some of the students do baby-sit—"

But Andie wasn't listening. Stiff with anger, she spun around and dashed from the office, her boot heels clomping loudly down the hall.

She couldn't believe it. This was a nightmare. After all their hard work. After all her planning. *It wasn't fair!*

"It's not fair!" Bursting through the exit doors, Andie shouted the words at the top of her lungs. Three students stopped to stare at her.

But she didn't care. She didn't care if the whole world thought she was nuts.

Andie raced up the hill to the stables, the cold wind stinging her eyes.

Without stopping, she grabbed Magic's halter and ran around the barn to the pasture. The Thoroughbred was grazing, but when he saw her his head popped up and he whinnied a greeting.

Andie halted by the gate, her breath coming in ragged gasps. She tried to whistle, but all that came out was a rush of air.

Tossing his head, Magic trotted across the grass to the fence. Quickly, Andie opened the gate. She rushed into the pasture, grabbed his mane, and buried her head in his neck.

"It's not fair!" she sobbed, her words muffled against his skin. "I don't care about those stupid grown-ups and their stupid rules. You're mine!"

Drawing back, Andie stared at Magic as he snuffled her fingers. He was so beautiful! Holding up the halter, she fumbled with the straps until she got it buckled on straight.

"Come on," she told him. "Let's go. We're leaving this place. I'll take you to Middlefield Stables. We'll live there together. I'll clean stalls for your board, and at night, I'll sleep in the straw and eat your grain."

Hooking the lead on the halter, she led him toward the gate.

"Andie!"

Andie glanced up. Mary Beth, Lauren, and Jina were jogging from the stables.

"Are you all right?" Lauren asked when they drew closer.

Andie nodded quickly. She halted Magic by the gate and started to unlatch it. Three Bars Jake ambled up beside her as if wondering what all the excitement was about.

"I'm just fine," Andie replied tersely. "In fact, I'm doing so good, I've decided to quit school. I was thinking of stealing Magic so I could take him with me, but then I realized what a dumb idea that was. Instead, I'll work at some stable until I earn enough money to buy him."

Swinging open the gate, she led Magic out. Her roommates stood in a line by the fence, staring at her.

"What are you guys looking at?" Andie snapped.

"You don't have to bite our heads off," Mary Beth snapped back. "We're just as mad as you. All that work for *nothing*."

"Really." Lauren shoved her hands hard into her coat pockets. "*We're* the ones who made beds and groomed horses and washed toilets and bagged snacks."

Jina nodded in agreement. "And cleaned tack. I can't believe I'm going to have to hand Ashley Stewart back that money. She's going to be so smug, it'll make me sick."

"Well, at least you two didn't get attacked by a horse," Mary Beth told Lauren and Jina. "That was the worst."

Lauren bristled. "Oh, yeah? I had to clean my sister's toilet. That was worse than the worst. That was disgusting."

"I'll tell you about disgusting—" Jina began.

Suddenly, Andie put two fingers in her mouth and let out an earsplitting whistle. Magic's head bobbed up, and Jake shied away from the gate.

"Hey, you guys!" Andie shouted angrily. "Listen to the three of you. Complaining about toilets and tack. I know that was a bum deal. But don't you get it? If my dad won't buy Magic, and *I* can't buy Magic, *he'll never be mine!*"

Her three roommates stopped arguing to look at her. Slowly, Jina shut her mouth. Tears began to glisten in Lauren's eyes, and Mary Beth's face fell.

"He'll never be mine," Andie repeated softly, the reality of her words suddenly hitting her. She stared unseeingly at her roommates. "I don't get it," she whispered. "This wasn't supposed to end this way. Magic was supposed to be mine."

Lauren bit back a sob. "You're right," she choked. "I can't believe how selfish we are." Stepping forward, she put her arm around Andie's shoulder. Mary Beth and Jina moved closer, too.

"I'm really sorry, Andie," Jina said.

For a moment, Andie drew away from her friends. Then a terrible feeling of sadness overwhelmed her. Her shoulders slumped in defeat. *It wasn't supposed to end this way.*

Covering her face with her hands, Andie burst into tears again. She couldn't bear to look over at Magic. It seemed as though her dream was finally over. For good.

Unless...Andie sniffed loudly, dried her eyes, and pulled herself a little straighter. She was never going to give up. She'd make Magic hers if it was the last thing she ever did. She'd show them all—her dad, Mrs. Caufield, Dean Wilkes—that they were making a big mistake.

Magic would belong to her. Someday.

Because Andie Perez would never give up.

Don't miss the next book in the Riding Academy series:
#10: TROUBLE AT FOXHALL

"Fawn is the most beautiful horse in the world!" Mary Beth exclaimed, patting the palomino's silky neck. She turned excitedly to Lauren. "I'd love to ride her for my lessons. Do you think Mrs. Caufield would assign her to me? I'm kind of sick of poky old Dan."

"Uh…" Lauren stammered.

"She's so *sweet*." Mary Beth laced her fingers through Fawn's cream-colored mane. "And she's got the most gorgeous golden color. Oh, I'll just die if I can't ride her!"

Lauren twisted her long blond braid. "Gee, Mary Beth, I hate to tell you this, but…you won't be able to ride Fawn."

Mary Beth spun around. "Why not?"

"Because…" Lauren bit her lip, then blurted out, "Because Mrs. Caufield assigned her to *me*."

ALISON HART has been horse-crazy since she was five years old. Her first pony was a pinto named Ted.

"I rode Ted bareback because we didn't have a saddle small enough," she says.

Now Ms. Hart lives and writes in Mt. Sidney, Virginia, with her husband, two kids, two dogs, one cat, her horse, April, and another pinto pony named Marble. A former teacher, she spends much of her time visiting schools to talk to her many Riding Academy fans. And you guessed it—she's still horse-crazy!